Perhaps sh

But Caitlin did would play arou her, a maturity... yet what qualifie to conclude all that? *He hardly knew her!*

The thoughts went round and round in his brain, making it impossible for him to get Caitlin out of his mind as he had resolved last night to do. It should have been easy. *He hardly knew her.* It *would* have been easy, Angus told himself, if it wasn't for Scott.

After living in the USA for nearly eight years, **Lilian Darcy** is back in her native Australia with her American historian husband and their three young children. More than ever, writing is a treat for her now, looked forward to and luxuriated in like a hot bath after a hard day. She likes to create modern heroes and heroines with good doses of zest and humour in their make-up, and relishes the opportunity that the medical series gives her for dealing with genuine, gripping drama in romance and in daily life. She finds research fascinating too—everything from attacking learned medical tomes to spending a day in a maternity ward.

Recent titles by the same author:

HER PASSION FOR DR JONES
TOMORROW'S CHILD
WANTING DR WILDE

THE COURAGE TO SAY YES

BY
LILIAN DARCY

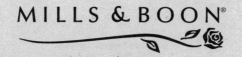

MILLS & BOON®

All the characters in this book have no existence outside the imagination of the author, and have no relation whatsoever to anyone bearing the same name or names. They are not even distantly inspired by any individual known or unknown to the author, and all the incidents are pure invention.

MILLS & BOON and MILLS & BOON with the Rose Device are registered trademarks of the publisher.

First published in Great Britain 1999
Harlequin Mills & Boon Limited,
Eton House, 18-24 Paradise Road, Richmond, Surrey TW9 1SR

© Lilian Darcy 1999

ISBN 0 263 81890 X

Set in Times Roman 10 on 11½ pt.
03-9912-54619-D

Printed and bound in Spain
by Litografia Rosés S.A., Barcelona

PROLOGUE

'SOMEONE close to my own age, who's perhaps been married before. Someone well travelled…' Gazing thoughtfully, as he spoke, into the middle distance of a warm Canberra afternoon in early summer, Angus Ferguson was startled to hear his sister Rachel's astonished hoot of laughter.

'My goodness, Angus, is that really what you think you're looking for in a life partner? A world-weary divorcee?'

'That's not what I said, is it?'

'Basically, yes.'

'I *didn't* say divorced.'

'You said someone who'd been married before. It's the same thing.'

'Well, I suppose I should have said someone who'd been—'

'Oh, so you mean a merry widow?'

'Rachel…'

'I'm afraid they're fairly thin on the ground in your age group. You're only thirty-five.'

'Now, little sister,' Angus returned firmly but rather indulgently, 'you were the one who asked me about my plans now that I was back in Australia—'

'Because, knowing you as I do, I knew there'd be some.'

'And I said I thought it was time to get serious about marriage—'

'Whereas normal people don't make any such decision. It simply hits them like a bolt from the blue.'

'And you asked me what sort of qualities I was looking for—'

'And you listed *attributes*, which isn't the same thing as *qualities* in the slightest.'

5

'And I attempted a serious answer to your question. I should have known I was wasting my time!'

But Angus wasn't really angry. He respected and valued Rachel's quirky insights very much. And he'd known quite well that he was presenting the whole issue in far too cut and dried a fashion. He found that helped, often, in clarifying sticky questions.

Rachel was still shaking her head at him, tut-tutting and smiling as she might have done at an incorrigible little boy, caught out for the umpteenth time in some harmless piece of mischief.

She looked very happy and very lazy this afternoon, sitting here on the timber deck of her house, with a tall glass of iced fruit juice within easy reach and her dark, wavy hair rippling around her shoulders. Thirty years old, and married to a man of whom Angus thoroughly approved, she was six months pregnant with their first child, and if she'd always given herself a broad licence to advise her elder brother on his personal life, impending motherhood only seemed to have made that licence even broader.

'Don't you remember what I've always told you about shopping for clothes?' she demanded now.

'Clothes?'

'Clothes, houses, wives. They're all the same,' she claimed extravagantly.

'Of course,' Angus drawled.

'When one's choice is largely a question of personal taste, you see, it's absolutely fatal to have too precise a list of requirements worked out in advance, and absolutely crucial to leave oneself open to being captivated by the completely unexpected.'

'I'm not sure that I fully grasp your point,' Angus returned gravely, stretching his bare legs out in front of him and lacing his fingers together behind his head.

He was thoroughly enjoying this lazy afternoon, doing noth-

ing more exhausting than allowing himself to be lectured by
his sister.

Wonderful to be back home, he thought, after several years
of Scottish and North American winters and summers, and far
too little time spent on things other than medicine.

In Rachel's spacious native bush garden, tall, shaggy-barked
gum-trees gave a dappled shade to the deck and currently
hosted several pairs of crimson rosellas. The golden wattle had
finished flowering months ago, but against a backdrop of grey-
green foliage, the red bloom of bottle-brush and grevillea gave
splashes of colour.

He took a gulp of his iced drink and watched Rachel lazily
as she searched for an apt clarification.

'Well, if I were buying a dress, for example...'

'A dress. OK.'

'And I'd convinced myself that I wanted something purple,
and ankle-length and with buttons down the front.'

'Right. Doesn't sound like *you*.' Rachel had Angus's own
colouring, with dark eyes and olive skin, and favoured pale
clothes of a casual cut. 'But go on!'

'I'd probably go to shop after shop and finally there it would
be, purple, ankle-length and buttons, and I'd be so pleased I
wouldn't think about the fact that the shade of purple was all
wrong and the fabric was some horrible cheap kind that would
pill at the elbows after two wearings. Meanwhile, there would
have been all sorts of other much lovelier dresses that I hadn't
considered because they didn't fit my superficial specifica-
tions.'

'I'm following you so far.'

'And if it's only a dress, it doesn't matter, of course, if it
turns out to be a mistake. But if it's a house or a wife...'

'Yes, well, a sensible man certainly doesn't want a wife
who pills at the elbows. I quite see that.'

'Angus, the point is—'

'Rachel, when I get beyond your unique way of stating your

case, the point is very clever and perceptive and true, and I can tell that you and Gordon bought this delightful house of yours in exactly that spirit.'

'Oh, we did!' she agreed. 'We told the real-estate agent we definitely wanted two bathrooms and a lock-up garage, and when we saw this place, open for exhibition, and fell in love with it on the spot, she was really quite cross with us because it doesn't have either!'

Angus let her get away for a few minutes longer with thinking he hadn't tumbled to where all this pretty chat about dresses and houses was ultimately leading, then finally took advantage of a brief silence and pounced.

'So you think I should abandon my preconceived divorcee?'

'Definitely!'

'And this wouldn't, by any chance, happen to be because you've got someone else in mind for me already?' he suggested silkily.

'Oh, Angus! Really!'

'Rachel…' he sang. 'I've known you for a long time now…'

'All right,' she admitted. 'All right, yes! I *do* have someone in mind. Gordon's sister, and she's lovely.'

'His sister? But I thought she was engaged. You told me so when you gave me her phone number in Sydney. I haven't phoned her yet…'

'You should. She's delightful. But I didn't mean *that* sister. Yes, Caitlin *is* engaged, more's the pity.' Angus almost queried this last phrase, but then let it slide. 'They're supposed to be getting married next year. No, I'm talking about Gordon's other sister. She's due back from overseas in a week, a little earlier than planned, she's unattached and you'll meet her at my in-laws' beach house when you come down for Christmas. She's a nurse at your new hospital, like Caitlin is. Her name's Erin…'

Again, Angus waited. Surely there would be more? A long catalogue of exaggerated virtues, probably, that would have

him sick of the very subject of Erin Gray before he'd even
met her. Surprisingly, however, Rachel said nothing further.
Perhaps motherhood was already adding to her store of human
wisdom and she'd realised it would be fatal to overstate her
case.

Instead, she changed the subject very briskly to ask, 'How
did your lecture go, by the way? I haven't asked.'

He frowned and shifted. 'Oh, fine…I think.' He'd spent the
morning in Newcastle, talking to a group of third-year medical
students about paediatric transplant surgery, and, after having
lunch there with a couple of colleagues, he'd seized on the
slightly extended weekend as an opportunity to fly down to
Canberra to see Rachel.

'You don't sound too convinced,' she probed. 'Caitlin's fiancé is just finishing his final year there. I hope it wasn't the
university that you had a problem with.'

'No, the lecture was fine,' he repeated, 'and most people
seemed interested, except one young rip who couldn't keep
his hands off his girlfriend the entire time and didn't even
have the decency to do it in the back row.'

Rachel laughed. 'Oh, Angus, you old prude! Presumably the
girlfriend wasn't paying too much attention to you either.'

'Well, that's a first!' he grinned back. 'No one's ever la-
belled me a prude before… But, no, she wasn't! And I simply
felt that if they were so very desperate to go to bed together—'

'My goodness, was it as hot and heavy as that?'

'Believe it! They should have left my lecture, found somewhere approximately horizontal and preferably private and got
on with it,'

'Have you no sympathy for young lovers?' she teased. 'Perhaps they didn't *have* anywhere private?'

'Rubbish!' he snorted, thinking back on the surf-blond male
student and his red-headed companion. *She* at least had managed to scribble a couple of notes. *He* hadn't even bothered

to take out a pen. 'It wasn't young love. It was blatant showing off, and I can't remember when I last had to work so hard to keep my concentration!'

'Oh, Angus,' Rachel laughed, reverting to the original thrust of their conversation. 'I think you're right in what you said earlier. It really is time you got yourself married!'

CHAPTER ONE

CAITLIN GRAY escaped onto the balcony of her parents' beach house and leaned on the wooden railing, watching the luminous evening sea.

Nice to take a break! It was just getting dark, and behind her the house was still in chaos. Dad and David were washing the vast mountain of dinner dishes. Mum was folding laundry. Peter was desperately searching the house for Binkie—the cuddly toy wombat without whom his two-year-old refused to go to sleep, and Robert was mopping the bathroom floor, which was at least a centimetre deep in water.

Caitlin herself had done sterling duty as an auntie, and had read five different bedtime stories to seven different nieces and nephews all under the age of ten. Her throat was quite tired from putting on different voices. Now the children's respective mothers—Caitlin's sisters-in-law Barbara, Sue and Lisa—were attempting to get them all calmed down enough to go to bed.

That would probably not be an easy task. It was Christmas Eve.

Caitlin had come down from Sydney by bus two days ago to enjoy a couple of peaceful days off and to help Mum prepare for the onslaught of family visitors. Christmas fell on a Friday this year, and she had to be back at work in one of Southshore Hospital's surgical wards, 6A, on Monday morning. Scott—her fiancé—would drive her back on Sunday afternoon, before heading another two hours north to Newcastle.

But it would be the last time he had to make the journey, and the last time they had to endure the distance and the separation. Scott had finished his medical course at Newcastle University now, and, despite having done less well in his studies than he'd hoped, was starting his internship at Sydney's Royal Prince Alfred Hospital in the New Year.

They wouldn't be sharing a place yet. Not until after their wedding, for which the date had still not been set. Caitlin would have been happy to share, but Scott thought her flat too small for two and not close enough to R.P.A. Which was all fine.

And yet the whole thing was unsettling somehow. They'd been involved for nearly four years. This should be a natural step. Scott was breezy and offhand about their future, but Caitlin was starting to want something more concrete. A wedding date, for example. She hated the fact that she hadn't seen him for so long, too. Almost six weeks, as he'd been so busy with final exams. It was ridiculous, of course, to think that things between them would have changed in that time…

Thinking about Scott, she pricked up her ears and went to the north end of the balcony from which, if she leaned out, she could just glimpse the road at the front of the house. A car was coming down the hill and slowing down, its headlights flooding into the gnarled banksia trees that stood just beyond the gravel verge.

The Grays' house, where her parents had lived since moving from Canberra after Dad's retirement last year, was the last one on this side of the road at the north end of Cargo Beach, before the road ducked up and away from the shore and headed towards the main highway.

Was this Scott? He could be here at any minute. Craning, she tried to make out the colour of the car, but it was too dark now. It could well be his, but on the other hand her fourth brother, Gordon, and his wife Rachel were expected tonight too. They were bringing Erin, who'd been staying with them in Canberra for ten days since getting back several weeks earlier than planned from overseas.

The car was definitely stopping. It lunged a little awkwardly off the road and into a gap in the banksias. Caitlin wondered why Scott wasn't using the driveway until she remembered how many cars were already parked there. It must be Scott, she had concluded. With lights from the houses across the road behind the car now, she could see that there was only one occupant, and could just make out the silhouette of a man's head above the steering-wheel.

Abandoning the peace and solitude of the balcony with some reluctance, she went back into the house to tell Mum he was here and then go out the front door to greet him.

Unfortunately, she failed in both missions. Lisa waylaid her in the corridor.

'Sorry, Caitlin, but could you *please* help Peter look for Binkie? Tyler's inconsolable. At home I might be firm with him, or manage to distract him or something, but down here… And this is the first time he's understood what Christmas means and he's *so* excited and over-tired. It's after nine! I'll never get him to sleep…'

'Of course I'll help.' She gave the frazzled Lisa a soothing pat on the arm. 'Has Peter tried in the garden?'

A knock at the front door punctuated her question, barely audible above Tyler's crying and David's and Barbara's older boys shrieking and laughing in the room next door. Poor Scott! He'd been heard to say before that the Grays' beach house at Christmas was a mad house. And he was right, of course.

She opened the door quickly to let him in, with an apology at the ready. 'Sorry… As usual, we're—'

It wasn't Scott at all. It was a total stranger, who looked nothing like him.

He had an imposingly broad-shouldered silhouette, naturally olive skin, dark and rather close-cropped hair, eyes as dark as a cat's at night and a craggy and almost forbidding face that somehow looked very familiar.

'Uh…hello,' he said in a gruff voice. 'Is this the Grays'? I'm—'

'Angus Ferguson,' Caitlin finished for him abruptly, as light dawned.

Rachel's brother. That's why he looked familiar. She had completely forgotten he was coming for Christmas as well. He'd been out of the country for several years, and his and Rachel's parents, who lived in Queensland, were away on an extended cruise this year. He'd had nowhere else to go.

'Please, come in!' she invited him in a flustered tone, still distracted by the noise and by the fact that he wasn't Scott. Seven-year-old Sean was grabbing her leg and giggling wildly.

'Uh, shall I—?' He was still standing in the doorway.

'I'm going *out*,' Caitlin clarified, politely attempting to get past him as she prised Sean loose and patted him on his messy, silky little head. 'To look for Binkie.'

'Binkie?'

'He's a wombat, and he's on the loose.'

'Good heavens!'

'No, sorry, a *toy* wombat, and Tyler won't go to sleep without him. Well, you can hear him. And— Oh! You're wondering about Rachel, of course, but she's not here yet. I expect they got a later start than planned, or something.'

'I expect so. Whereas perhaps I'm a little too early.'

'I'm sorry, this must be—'

'It's fine,' he assured her seriously. 'But it seems to me that the obvious thing for me to do, rather than bringing in my luggage or attempting to introduce myself to your parents, is to help you find Binkie.'

She seized on the suggestion with relief. '*Would* you? Wonderful! Because it's pointless your trying to get settled and meet everyone at this stage.'

'I can see that,' he drawled, and his face spread into a heart-stopping smile.

Startled at the way it softened his face so dramatically, Caitlin locked her gaze to his and there was a giddy beat of silence. Until that moment she hadn't really looked at him.

Not properly. Not for more than half a second as her flustered gaze shifted between the chaos behind her in the bedroom and the dark tranquillity of the evening outside.

Now it was as if the universe had suddenly and quite silently tilted. She felt as if her body no longer belonged to her, her strength was gone, and for several long seconds she had absolutely no idea what she was doing with her limbs or her voice or her eyes.

The silent earthquake feeling very soon settled into a strange sort of calm, and she was able to think distantly, This is odd… Is it just the surprise of seeing Rachel's face in such a masculine form? But he mustn't see that anything has happened. That would be just too…too silly. I must behave quite normally.

He was still looking at her, his body held in an attitude of receptive stillness, as if he could hear some far-off music and was straining to catch the melody. Caitlin said thinly and too quickly, 'I'm wondering if Binkie's been left in the garden. I was on my way out to check when you rang the bell.'

'It looks like a big garden.'

'It is. You can hardly tell where it ends and the beach begins.'

'I have a torch in my car.'

'That's a good idea. It's very dark under the trees, despite the moon. I'll find a torch, too.'

A perfectly ordinary and very practical conversation. Beyond it, however, something else was going on. Caitlin's ears were ringing, and her brain felt as if it had been stuffed with cotton wool. Her nerve-endings, on the other hand, were vibrantly receptive. Going in search of a torch, she shook off the feeling angrily, disturbed at its intensity.

She'd been hearing this man's praises from his sister for two years, but hadn't expected to find him quite so instantly compelling. She should have done, perhaps, since he was a very highly regarded paediatric surgeon.

She and Angus met at the foot of the steps a minute later, and he said something light and silly about search parties. Caitlin laughed, delighted and relieved. Being Rachel's brother, he couldn't help having a sense of humour. He would hardly have survived childhood with his sibling if he hadn't! It was a critical quality in any human being, Caitlin considered, and there was an extra appeal in it when it came from someone so outwardly forbidding of aspect and so obviously intelligent.

'And I vote you as expedition co-ordinator,' he added now, 'since you'll have the most accurate information as to where the missing hiker was last seen.'

'Hiker?'

'It's usually a hiker, isn't it? Except at sea. Then it's a lone yachtsman. What colour is he?'

'Binkie? Wombat-coloured, unfortunately,' she answered.

'Ah!' he drawled. 'A nocturnal animal, designed to be well camouflaged in the bush after dark.'

'Yes, neon green would have helped, wouldn't it? Oh, well, we have the torches. I think Tyler was playing over here just before tea.'

She waved her torch beam at the banksias between the house and the beach and they searched diligently there for several minutes, gradually moving farther apart and giving short reports to each other at intervals.

'Not here,' he said.

'No. Perhaps I'll try the other side of the bushes,' she answered. From the corner of her eye she was very conscious of the strong silhouette of his body and the decisive way he moved.

'OK, and I'll come around in an arc towards you...'

Caitlin had heard a nursing colleague speak of the camaraderie and closeness that grew very quickly amongst search and rescue workers. She hadn't expected to feel it when scouring a beach-side garden for a missing toy animal.

They had no luck.

'I think he's returned to the wild to join his wombat brothers,' Angus decided cheerfully.

'They've probably been planning his break-out for months,' Caitlin agreed, and they both laughed again.

'Did Tyler treat him well? Did he have any incentive to escape?'

'Tyler treated him terribly! He's already had his seams mended twice.'

'Then perhaps we should turn traitor to our mission and leave him to his freedom.'

'Well, I'm not sure that that falls within a devoted auntie's brief, but certainly for tonight I've had enough,' she agreed.

Looking up at the house, Caitlin saw that it seemed quieter now, and the light was off in Tyler's and Alice's room. And wasn't this Lisa coming out onto the balcony?

'What's happening, Lisa?' she called. 'I'm afraid we can't find Binkie out here.'

'Oh, no!' Lisa wailed. 'Didn't anybody tell you? We found him ten minutes ago. He was in Tyler's cot all the time, hidden under the bottom of his quilt.'

'Lisa!' Caitlin groaned, above Angus Ferguson's dry chuckle just a few feet from her. She heard a click as he switched off his torch, and did the same herself. 'You didn't realise we were still looking?'

'No. I'm really sorry…'

'I think you'll owe Angus for some torch batteries.'

'Rachel's brother? I didn't even realise he was here… Oh, and your mother just said she can hear another car arriving.'

She disappeared inside again, while Caitlin noted the car headlights turning in from the road beyond the house and thought, Scott!

Angus, at the same time, had obviously thought, Rachel!

Each having made a different decision about which way to go around the house, they set off in the dark without looking and cannoned into each other. Caitlin was knocked off balance and might have fallen if Angus hadn't grabbed her arm and shored her up. Not in perfect control himself, he hauled her roughly against his chest and she gasped.

'Whoops!' he muttered, and he should have released her straight away, but he didn't.

Instead, he held her for three seconds too long, so that she could feel the way her breasts pressed against his pale blue shirt and learned exactly how much she had to tilt her head to look up at him. That ringing sound was back in her ears, and her brain felt woollier than ever.

'All right?' he growled, letting her go very slowly.

'Fine,' she answered breathlessly, hugging herself in a defensive gesture.

'Good. I'm so sorry.' His tone was gruff now. He'd noticed her stiffness.

'It was as much my fault as yours,' she insisted.

'Was it?'

'Yes. Neither of us…looked before we leapt.'

There was a beat of silence. They'd all been such conventional words. So why did they seem so significant?

'It's a beautiful night,' he said finally, turning to look at the ocean. 'Later on, when I've met everyone and we've all got settled, would you like to show me the beach?'

'I—'

Was there any reason why she should say no? There was, only she couldn't summon it for the moment. Showing him the beach would be an act of politeness, if nothing else, as he was her sister-in-law's brother.

But she suddenly remembered why she couldn't agree. Scott was due to arrive, and they'd be spending the rest of the evening together. In fact…

'Caitlin?' called her mother. 'Scott's here, love.'

Angus stepped back abruptly. He had been standing quite close. 'Caitlin? You're *Caitlin*!'

'Yes.' She nodded. 'You mean after all this I've forgotten to even introduce myself? I'm sorry. It—it doesn't *matter*, does it?' she added uncertainly.

Even in the cool blue light of the moon she could see that he looked taken aback, almost shocked.

A second later she doubted her impression. He was saying lightly, 'Matter? Of course not. I just feel a little stupid, that's all. I made the assumption you were driving down with your fiancé. That is, I didn't think you were *you* at all, and—' He broke off and swore under his breath. 'I thought you were Erin,' he finished woodenly. 'Purely my mistake. And, of course, it's not important.'

'No,' she agreed politely. How could it be? 'Erin is coming down with your sister. Tonight. I've been here for two days.'

'Right' He nodded. 'Typical Rachel. A crucial detail, carelessly omitted.'

He ought to have been smiling. Caitlin had understood from her mother, and from Rachel herself, that Angus was an excellent elder brother, very fond of his sister and rather indulgent towards her. But he wasn't smiling, and she was reminded of the first impression she'd had of his forbidding face.

'Caitlin, that *is* you out there, isn't it?' her mother called again.

'Yes, Mum,' she called back.

'Because poor Scott's struggling with presents and his duffel bag.'

'Of course. I'll help.' She turned to Angus. 'I'm sorry,' she said again, although she didn't know quite what she was apologising for.

'No problem,' he growled. 'Forget it. Please!'

She nodded and turned away to go and greet her fiancé, wondering why her stomach felt so churned up all of a sudden.

'What a bloody idiot I was not to *ask*!' Angus muttered to himself as he ducked under the brittle leaves of a banksia branch on the way to his car.

It really wasn't important, of course. Or it shouldn't be. For twenty minutes he'd thought he was feeling a quite startlingly sudden attraction to a very eligible woman who was not only unattached but who had been personally recommended to him by his own sister.

And now he'd discovered himself to be wrong on all counts. End of story. Caitlin Gray *wasn't* unattached, and she *wasn't* the woman Rachel had focused her matchmaking sights upon. Even the attraction, surely, had to have been opportunism and very little else.

He had only got one clear view of her, as she'd stood there in the doorway with the light of the corridor behind her, looking delightfully fidgety and flushed and flustered, with her blonde ponytail half pulled down by a child's busy fingers so that the escaped wavy strands made a halo around her face, and her blue eyes eager and apologetic and distractedly roving by turns.

Funny how it was the little things that counted, though. When he'd assumed her to be Erin, he'd felt quite self-satisfied about that—about his own perception. He'd noted how she'd managed to keep talking to him while a seven-year-old grabbed her leg, not shaking the urchin nephew off, or snapping cross words at him, but just giving him a tender, absent pat on the head.

A little later, out in the garden, he'd noted the responsiveness of her laugh, how diligently she'd searched, bending and stretching her slender figure, and how even Lisa's belated announcement of the successful discovery of Binkie had created only one moment of mild and honestly aired annoyance before she'd shrugged it off quite cheerfully.

In view of all this, perhaps it was hardly surprising that she was already spoken for. No doubt the unknown Scott deserved her, too. Angus wished them joy. And he'd probably be invited to the wedding.

No thanks were owing to Rachel on this occasion, however.

'I'll tell her when I get a chance—no more matchmaking on my behalf, thanks!' he growled, shoving the torch into his glove-box and snapping it shut. 'If she hadn't put the idea of Erin into my head in the first place, I'd never have got myself into this position!'

What 'position', though? The thing was finished. You couldn't possibly fall in love with someone in the space of twenty minutes. He would look forward, in a very mild and cautious way, to meeting the real Erin instead.

Although, after what had just happened, he would swear off any temptation to consider her as having any possible connection with his own future. Rachel was right about one thing. It was very dangerous, he now saw, to *plan* to fall in love.

Again he shook off the idea. He hadn't planned any such thing! Rachel always teased him with the notion that his plans were coldly made and set in stone but that wasn't really so, and they both knew it.

He hadn't wanted to marry young because he'd seen so many youthful marriages involving doctors flounder and fail badly. But if the right woman had come along during those training days he wouldn't have closed off the idea out of some cautious principle.

In the event, it hadn't happened. There had been two women he'd come close with, but one was wedded to her career and the other... Well, what was the term she'd used for what they had shared for three months? 'Transitional relationship.' That's right. She'd just finalised her divorce and Angus had belatedly discovered that he'd been a stage in her therapy more than anything else.

Now he knew that the time was right for him to marry, if he was ever going to, but he wasn't in any hurry. He'd seen enough to know that the right relationship didn't just fall into your lap. Most people had to work at it, and you couldn't simply will it into being...

Swinging two suitcases—mainly containing presents—out

of the boot, he made his way back towards the house to run the gauntlet of belated introductions, feeling a little grim and solitary. But he found that things had calmed down considerably, and the noise came from the adults rather than the children now.

Rachel, Gordon and Erin had arrived and he encountered them on the front stairs. He kissed Rachel, shook Gordon's hand, felt his mood lift again and managed a suitable greeting to Erin, who looked like an older version of twenty-three-year-old Caitlin, only much less vibrant.

Then he fetched up in the big, open-plan living area to meet the rest of the family, and there in all his tanned, blond and handsome glory was 'my fiancé, Scott Sinclair', as Caitlin introduced him, already known to Angus as the young surf-god who had distracted him from his lecture three weeks ago in Newcastle.

They shook hands.

They locked startled, wary glances.

Angus drawled deliberately, 'Somehow, I feel I've met you somewhere before, Scott.' Then he immediately wondered why he'd dared the man in that way. It wasn't to test his own memory on the issue. Having spent an hour trying to avoid looking at the ardent young lover, he was quite certain this was the same person. On the other hand, the redhead with the notepad had definitely not been Caitlin.

Scott Sinclair, meanwhile, had recovered his cool and seemed quite unfazed by the veiled attack. 'Not met, exactly,' he replied easily. 'I was at your lecture on transplant surgery a few weeks ago, although I didn't manage to catch your name that day. No idea you were Rachel's brother.'

'I see…'

'Excellent presentation, by the way.' The social lie was glib and bold-faced and quite shameless. 'Fascinating!'

'Did you take notes?'

'Well, no, I'm not a third-year student, you see.'

'Yes, I was going to ask about that.' Angus nodded calmly. 'You've just finished your final year, haven't you?'

'Yes, but you know how it is…'

'I'm not sure that I do.'

'When there's someone really…interesting…you find you just can't keep away. Sometimes, the third years have the best of what's on offer.'

'Really? Just the third years?'

'Well, I have moved a bit beyond first year…er…anatomy these days…' Scott grinned, as if to say, Let's face it, we're both men of the world, and aren't I witty about it, too?

Angus's gut boiled with disgust and he nodded silently. As he'd told Rachel, he hadn't been too impressed with the man's behaviour at the time. Now it had acquired a much uglier twist. Caitlin's fiancé was a womaniser. Did she have any idea?

She was standing right beside Scott, listening to all this, her wide, pretty mouth curved in an increasingly uncertain smile. Scott had actually snaked his arm around her as he was crafting those unsubtle double entendres. Had Caitlin picked up on them? Evidently not, although she was frowning now…

Feeling Scott's arm sliding more closely around her waist, Caitlin glanced uneasily between the two men. Angus Ferguson was bristling with tension, and Scott, although he was still grinning his lazy, heart-stopping grin, was holding himself with tight wariness. She could feel it in his body, pressed against hers.

And there had been something…odd…about that conversation. It wasn't nearly as casual as it appeared. She'd have to ask Scott about it later when they were alone. Now was not the time. Angus still hadn't been introduced to her parents, and Rachel was pulling him away. Scott had a question for her, too.

'How come your mother hasn't put us in the same room?' he muttered irritably to Caitlin.

'Because she has her rules, Scott. I know it seems old-fashioned to you…'

'You got that right! I thought now that we were actually engaged we'd pass.'

'Not until we're married, I'm afraid.' She made a face, trying to keep it light, but she felt uncomfortable at the fact that he was making an issue of it. She caught a glance—possibly sympathetic?—from Rachel and hoped her sister-in-law couldn't hear this.

'Maybe I could talk her round. If I tell her we've set the date—'

'But we haven't,' she pointed out steadily. Scott had always been a highly sexed man, and tended to lose perspective when he was thwarted. 'And I don't want you to "talk her round". It's her rule and this is her house, and I respect that, even though, yes, she knows perfectly well that we—'

'She won't even *know*, Caitlin. Your parents' bedroom is at the other end of the house. We haven't slept together since you came up in November. That's nearly seven weeks ago! You've got to ask Erin to—'

'No, Scott,' she finished quietly. 'I—I know we haven't had much time together, but we just have to be patient. If for no other reason, you can't possibly expect Erin and Angus to share!'

He dropped the subject finally, but it set a sour tone to the evening. There had been a few such tensions between them lately. Since they had got engaged several months ago, in fact. It was a difficult state to be in, Caitlin considered. A sort of limbo. Especially since for the past six weeks they'd only had the phone. Things would be much easier when they were married.

CHAPTER TWO

CHRISTMAS in summer. Part of Caitlin's earliest memories. They'd had a beach house here since she was three, although when she was twelve the old fibro cottage had been bulldozed and this much grander and lovelier house put up instead. Sited at the north end of pleasantly wild Cargo Beach, it had a wide balcony that looked over the water, a huge open-plan kitchen, living and dining room and lots of cubbyhole bedrooms for grandchildren and guests.

On Christmas morning the grandchildren were up early, demanding their presents. Caitlin got up too, not wanting to miss the excitement, although four feet away by the window Erin lay asleep on her stomach, clearly intending to stay that way.

Caitlin had been shocked at the change in her sister last night, seeing her for the first time since she had departed happily for a working holiday in England almost a year ago. Erin looked strained and unhappy and thin.

Caitlin had whispered to Mum, just before going to bed, 'What's wrong with Erin?'

'I wish I knew. She won't say. All I know is that it involves a man. Caitlin, if you can get her to talk about it, please, do!'

And Caitlin had tried to engineer a heart-to-heart last night when they'd been lying here in the dark in their twin beds, but she hadn't had any more success than Mum. There was a man involved, and it was a hopeless mess, and Erin was miserable.

'But I don't want to talk about it. *Please*, don't ask, OK?'

'OK, Erin.'

Now Erin buried her blonde head deeper into the pillow and groaned. Obviously, she needed her rest.

Scott and Angus must have needed theirs, too, as there was no sign of either of them and their bedroom door was firmly closed.

This made Caitlin feel pleasantly relaxed. She didn't have to play hostess. She didn't have to deal with Scott's inevitable moodiness when he was with her family. She could please herself and enjoy the morning.

She grabbed a thirty-second shower and put on navy linen shorts and a matching striped T-shirt, then brewed coffee for herself and various tired parents as seven children of various sizes noisily explored the contents of their Christmas stockings. It was a delightful half-hour.

'But all the other presents have to wait until *after* breakfast.' That was the unified verdict of the three sets of parents. It was still barely seven o'clock. The children took a bit of persuading. There was still a large and tantalising pile beneath the tree.

After a few wails and protests, though, they were persuaded to look favourably at breakfast, so Caitlin made more coffee for herself and a serving of cereal and wandered onto the balcony to eat at the table there and watch the morning sun on the sea…at which point she received quite a shock.

Angus Ferguson wasn't safely in bed at all. He was sitting out here with a book. He wore shorts that revealed bare, very brown legs with dark hair, and he was absently tickling the golden forehead of Margot, Mum's and Dad's middle-aged Labrador.

And Margot was loving it.

Caitlin stopped in her tracks and Angus looked up casually so that the sun struck on his dark head and brought out unexpected highlights of molten gold. He gave a frown at her startled expression.

'Is reading before breakfast not allowed?' he queried gruffly, with only the ghost of a reluctant, crooked smile to soften his craggy face.

'No, I—I mean, of course it is, but…I thought you were still asleep. Scott, too.'

'Scott is,' he answered. 'At least, he was when I got up, and since then I've done a fairly thorough prowl down to the beach and around the garden, with this charming new lady friend of mine…'

At which point Margot simply rolled onto her back, presented her pale, honeycomb-coloured tummy and seemed to say, Take me! Neither the man nor the dog seemed to realise that females were supposed to play hard to get.

'And I haven't spotted him.'

'Heavens!' Caitlin blurted. 'What time were you up?'

'Before six,' he admitted on a drawl. 'It's such a beautiful hour at this time of year, and with the sun rising over the water, so bright and already warm…'

Caitlin privately agreed, but wasn't going to take the risk of saying so. Somehow she felt that discovering anything in common with this man would be very dangerous. He disturbed her, with his rough-hewn masculinity, so different from Scott's golden good looks, and she didn't like the feeling. The two men seemed to have taken an immediate dislike to each other, and she knew where her loyalty lay. With Scott, of course.

Attempting to disguise what she felt, she said in an over-bright tone, 'But you've been hiding yourself out here. You haven't been able to eat.'

'Not hiding,' he corrected. 'It's great out here. And I'd have eaten if I'd wanted to. I just didn't want to get in the way of the present fest.'

'Oh, you wouldn't have,' she assured him.

Somewhat guiltily she realised that it was only decent of her to make Angus Ferguson feel welcome. He was Rachel's brother. Almost family.

Rachel had used the word herself some weeks ago. 'May I give Angus your phone number, Caitlin?' she'd asked over the phone from Canberra. 'He has colleagues in Sydney, but you're more like family and he may appreciate that.' Then she'd added with a hint of reluctance, 'He's taking up quite a senior position at Southshore, too, so you never know, it may be helpful for Scott to get to know him.'

Angus hadn't phoned, though, and now Caitlin was quite glad of the fact.

'We're all *very* relaxed here, you know,' she appended, fighting to find the right tone with him. It shouldn't be so hard!

'I know that, Caitlin.' Her name sounded both crisp and fluid in his rather dark voice. He put down his book and she noticed his fine, perfectly controlled surgeon's hands. For a man who was very definitely not good-looking—far too rough-hewn, she'd already decided that—there was a strange magnetism to his body. 'I really can take care of myself, you know.'

That slow smile softened his mouth and eyes, but didn't break fully into his face as it had done last night. He wasn't going out of his way to impress this morning. There was a definite change.

Or is it just me?

She flushed. 'Of course you can. I'm sorry…'

'Look, would it make you feel better to bring me a coffee?' Hell, he'd noticed her odd behaviour! 'I don't know where everything is kept yet,' he explained reasonably.

The 'yet' was ominous. It reminded Caitlin that Rachel might very easily pull her brother into the Gray family circle on a permanent basis as their own parents lived so far away. Quite possibly, she'd meet him down here or in Canberra several times a year, not to mention running into him at Southshore. She found the prospect daunting, and said far too heartily, 'Coming right up, sir!' Then she felt like a fool.

In the kitchen she realised she hadn't asked him how he wanted it, but took a gamble and made it the way she liked it herself—fairly strong, but with lots of scalded milk, in a very big mug—rather than meekly trotting back out to the balcony to clarify the issue.

'Ah…!' he said a moment later, and his eyes lit up as his fingers cradled the mug and his finely drawn nostrils took in the rich scent. 'This looks perfect!'

Caitlin settled down in a chair, facing the sea as he was and close enough to talk but not *too* close. Now, should she ask him a couple of questions about himself or keep to neutral topics? Perhaps silence was safest. She sensed that he was a man who didn't enjoy talking merely for the sake of avoiding silence.

But here was Rachel, before Caitlin had had a chance to say anything at all. She was relieved at her sister-in-law's arrival at first. Rachel certainly wouldn't feel awkward with her own brother.

Rachel failed to provide the hoped-for relief, however. She looked very droopy in her tent-like sundress today, unlike her normal vibrant self, and Caitlin saw that she was holding her pregnant stomach rather fretfully.

Angus noticed it, too.

'Rachel?' he demanded. 'There's nothing wrong, is there?'

'You're the doctor, Angus,' Rachel retorted from beneath a dark brown fringe that needed cutting. 'You tell me.'

'You mean you think there might be something?' He set his coffee down abruptly.

'I don't know!' She sat down, then immediately stood up again.

'Well?' he prompted.

'I'm having pains…I think. But, you know, all those descriptions in the pregnancy books can't *really* express what it's like. Maybe this is something I ate.'

'How long since they started?'

'Just before I got up.'

'Oh, Rachel,' Caitlin cut in. 'That's an hour ago! And you

didn't say anything while the kids were opening their presents?'

'Well, you know, I didn't want to spoil it.'

Angus uncoiled himself from his chair, put his arm gently around his sister and said quietly, 'Remind me, Rachel, when exactly are you due?'

'Not for nine weeks…'

'Then let's get you to hospital. There's no sense taking a risk.'

Rachel promptly burst into tears, and Caitlin's insides flipped at that ominous word 'risk'. All the many cheerful obstetric experiences she'd ever had or heard of during the midwifery part of her training went flying out of her memory and only the rare unhappy ones remained. If Angus hadn't retained his total calm…

'Get her down to my car,' he told Caitlin briefly, his dark eyes locked on hers. 'Have her lie in the back on her left side with her feet on a pillow. I'll tell Gordon, and he can tell people what's going on and follow along. Let's not cause a general panic because it may be a false alarm. Premature labour can often be halted if action is taken soon enough. Of course you'd know that. There *is* a hospital near here, right, Rachel? Didn't I notice it shortly before I turned off the highway?'

'Yes, in Houghton,' Rachel answered. 'But it's so small!'

'No, they've got a new A and E department now,' Caitlin soothed her. 'I'm sure they're very well equipped.'

'Good,' Angus nodded, and disappeared into the house.

Caitlin helped a shaky Rachel down the stairs that ran directly into the garden from the south end of the balcony.

'I don't want to lose this baby…' Rachel said.

'Of course not. And you won't.'

'I didn't take it seriously until Angus talked about risks.'

'I know.'

'Do you think he knows something that he's not saying?'

'He's…he's a paediatric surgeon, Rachel,' Caitlin reminded her weakly. 'He's…seen a lot.' Including surgical problems that were the direct result of babies being born too soon. Unfairly, she felt a spurt of anger at Rachel's brother. Couldn't he have played this down? It was Christmas Day!

Which would be a *great* day to lose a baby! she realised. No, Angus could not have played it down.

He reappeared before she had finished helping Rachel into the car, carrying the pillow he'd mentioned, and there was something intensely reassuring in the purposeful way he moved and in the steady set of his mature, rather strong-featured face. In those brief shorts his thighs looked as hard as two logs of wood.

'Are you comfortable like that?' he asked Rachel.

'Y-yes.'

'And there's been no bleeding or other fluid?'

'No.'

'Any mucus?'

'No.'

'That's all good news, Rachel.' He squeezed her shoulders. 'Your cervix may well not be dilating at all. Hang in there. The hospital will handle this, and there's every chance it will be stopped.'

'I—I hope so. But why, Angus? I mean, I haven't done anything strenuous. What's gone wrong?'

'It could be any one of a number of things,' Angus said, as he started the car and manoeuvred it into the street. 'The most likely one is probably an infection in the urinary tract or cervix.'

'You mean…' Rachel stopped and thought for a moment. 'Actually, I have been running to the bathroom a lot the past couple of days. I thought it was just the baby pressing on my bladder. And then last night and this morning it really stung. I never made the connection—Oh, here's another contraction… Oh, will everything be all right?'

It was only a ten-minute journey—even less on Christmas Day and at the speed Angus drove in his sleek, dark green car. Caitlin sat twisted around in the front seat, chafing Rachel's hand in her own.

At the hospital things were blessedly quiet, although this meant there was no doctor on the spot and the one who was on call had to come in from home. She arrived within five minutes, by which time Rachel was already gowned and in bed, again with feet elevated and on her left side, and a nurse was preparing to set up a drip and take a urine sample.

Angus quickly identified himself as her brother. He then even more quickly listed his professional credentials, which Caitlin found humbling. She knew Rachel was proud of her brother, and had immediately sensed his intelligence herself, but hadn't realised he'd trained and worked on three continents.

Finally, he explained the situation and handed over his temporary medical authority to the brisk, pleasant English GP, Dr Mann.

'Right,' she said. 'Sounds like we should examine you, Mrs Gray, and pop you on a monitor. If there is evidence of infection in your urine, we'll start you on a safe antibiotic straight away and we'll have a thorough check for any other causes, too.'

Angus and Caitlin left the room while Dr Mann did a quick internal exam. She called them back a minute later to report, 'Mrs Gray's mucus plug is still intact. There's no evidence of bleeding, and the cervix isn't dilated.' Then, to Rachel herself, she said 'There's no effacement—thinning—of the cervix either, Mrs Gray. I'm sure we can convince this baby that Christmas *isn't* the best day of the year to be born in the present instance!'

'Oh… Oh, thank goodness! Oh, I hardly dare to believe it!' Rachel turned to Caitlin and Angus. 'Thanks… I'm shaking now. Isn't that stupid? Can you stay until Gordon—?'

But Gordon was here already. 'No one's panicking,' he reported in his quiet, steady way. 'Mum's worried, of course. Wants to come and see you, but doesn't think she'll have time, what with the salads for lunch and the turkey for dinner.'

'As to that,' Angus said confidently at once, 'there are four healthy single adults under her roof. Will Scott and Erin pitch in, do you think, Caitlin?'

'I'm sure they will. Scott's not much of a cook.'

'Neither am I but, as a surgeon, I do have a certain talent for cutting and peeling…'

Rachel shuddered, then giggled.

Angus's grin was unrepentant. 'You looked like you needed a laugh.'

'And that's the best you could come up with?'

'Limited resources at the moment.'

'Well, anyway, shoo!' Rachel said. 'After turning my stomach like that, you can give me a moment alone with Caitlin.'

'Sure…' If he was curious about the request, it didn't show. He just loped from the room, still grinning.

Catlin was curious herself, but Rachel put her out of her misery pretty quickly. 'This is so annoying!' she moaned. 'You see, I have a little plan for bringing Angus and Erin together. Don't you think it could work, Caitlin? They're both well travelled, both have medical careers and I know Angus is ready to settle down. Could you possibly try to get them to go for a swim together, or leave them all the Christmas dishes to wash on their own, or something?'

Her eagerness was endearing and funny, but there was no use in raising false hopes.

'I don't think Erin is in the market at the moment, Rachel,' Caitlin told her sadly.

'You mean this rotten man in England?'

'Yes. Has she told you?'

'Only that she didn't want to talk about it.'

'Same here. So don't you think…?'

'But Angus will *cure* her of him, Caitlin!'

'Oh, I don't think Erin's like that, Rachel, I really don't. I very much doubt she could hop straight from one man to another. Like a…like a flea or something. I know *I* couldn't…'

Rachel's face fell in disappointment. She was such a warm, eager person, always promoting the best for other people, usually with such huge enthusiasm that the people concerned were lucky to escape unscathed. Caitlin considered her a very entertaining addition to the Gray family, and applauded Gordon's taste.

'I suppose you're right,' Rachel admitted. 'I thought… I mean, Erin has had *two weeks*, and Angus is just *the best* person under that serious façade of his.'

Caitlin hid her smile, kissed her sister-in-law and took her leave.

Angus was waiting for her along the corridor. 'All sorted out?'

'Yes, though Rachel's a bit disappointed,' Caitlin said absently. She had been absorbed, as she approached him, in trying to work out just what was so imposing about his presence that it drew her eye so relentlessly. Was it just the instinctive confidence and authority that any successful surgeon had?

'Disappointed?' he queried.

She realised too late that she couldn't possibly explain what she really meant, and improvised quickly, 'Well, about missing Christmas, of course.'

'Right.' He nodded, jiggling his car keys in his hand.

They walked to the car side by side in silence, and didn't speak again until he pulled up in her parents' driveway.

'I'm glad it's a cold lunch.' Angus broke the silence finally as they got out of the car. 'That sky is so bright now that it's burning.'

'Did you miss that overseas?' Caitlin asked before she could stop herself. As she was very determined to remain aloof from him, it didn't exactly make sense to ask open-ended questions.

'People say that nowhere else in the world has skies as blue as ours,' she finished, hoping he'd find a brief reply.

'It's true, too,' he said. 'I even missed our incongruous summer Christmas, much as I enjoyed the experience of snow in the US. But, tell me, speaking of summer Christmases, how do the Gray family like their salads?'

They reached the front door.

'Oh…light and lively,' she answered, not really caring what she was saying. 'We usually try something a bit different each year. Mum has a new recipe this year for one with beetroot, walnut and chives.'

'Hmm… Not for the children?' he suggested.

So it became—in many people's minds anyway—'the Christmas that Rachel was in Houghton Hospital', and Mum didn't touch the turkey until a serving of it reached her plate at seven that night. A surprisingly delightful day, Caitlin considered. Rachel did have a urinary tract infection and was started on antibiotics, and though the contractions were real they ebbed gradually once she was safely on bedrest so that the family's anxiety about the baby was only slight.

Angus was reassuring, too, in his initial report to Mum. 'As long as she takes things easy and is alert for any signs of further trouble, she'll probably carry it to term,' he explained, responding to a barrage of anxious questions. 'They'll teach her today how to monitor her own contractions with her fingertips when they're so slight that she wouldn't be aware of them if she was moving around, and her doctor in Canberra will probably want to check her urine more often than is routine. I imagine Dr Mann will discharge her tomorrow.'

Scott and Erin rose at nine and nine-thirty respectively, to be greeted with the news that Rachel's baby was threatening an early arrival, Mum had gone to sit with her and they'd been volunteered *in absentia* for the cooking team. The four of them then produced a commendable array of salads to augment the luxurious cold seafood platter and carved ham joint, as well as making an enormous batch of turkey stuffing and peeling the vegetables ready for baking later this afternoon.

Lunch was noisy and served buffet-style. Most adults sat out on the balcony to eat, while children picked at the minimum they could get away with, being still too absorbed in new toys to feel hungry.

Speaking of new toys, Scott had given Caitlin a tiny music-box which played a Strauss waltz and revealed an elegantly dressed couple dancing in the snow when the lid was opened. It was sweet and expensive and very pink and didn't reflect her taste at all, and as she suspected that she hadn't hidden this fact quite well enough she was remorsefully solicitous of his welfare all through the meal. He never seemed much at home amongst all the family noise. Perhaps it was hardly surprising. There were eighteen of them, even with Mum and Rachel and Gordon at the hospital.

About the only other thing Caitlin had time to notice as they ate was that, at the far end of the balcony, Dad and Angus seemed to be getting on famously. Well, Dad adored Rachel after all.

When lunch was finished, Angus, Erin, Scott and Caitlin tackled the dishes, while the other adults entertained children or put them off for naps.

'And now, I think,' said Angus at two o'clock, 'we've got time for a swim.'

Which was really the thing that made it an Australian beach Christmas, as far as Caitlin was concerned—the absurd and familiar contrast between all the winter-orientated rituals and the hedonistic splendour of the heat. Just why did most Australians feel compelled to eat a full roast dinner on a hot summer day? As Angus had said earlier, the very incongruousness of it was part of the tradition.

The water was glorious, and Scott matched Caitlin wave for wave as they surfed with lightweight boogie boards for almost an hour. After a shorter swim Angus invited Erin to walk with him down to the far end of the beach.

'I expect Scott and Caitlin would appreciate a bit of peace, and I'd like the exercise.'

Erin accepted, but as the two figures dwindled in the distance Caitlin could see that her sister wasn't providing much companionship. She was walking at least five metres from Angus, splashing her feet in the shallows and watching the waves.

'Do you like Rachel's brother?' Scott asked idly half an hour later, observing their return from the vantage point of his towel spread on the hot sand.

'He seems like good fun.' Caitlin made a deliberately colourless reply to his question. For some reason she didn't want to discuss Angus. Not with Scott or anyone else.

There was a pause. 'I don't.' Scott scowled.

'No, I guessed that,' Caitlin said cautiously. 'Why?'

'Oh, just the sort of pompous, self-righteous type I detest, that's all.'

'But how can you possibly know that about him so quickly?'

Scott shrugged. 'Doctors have to be perceptive about people.'

'Some of them aren't!' Including Scott himself? Angus hadn't seemed to her to be pompous or self-righteous at all.

'Well, anyway…'

'What happened at that lecture?' she probed, remembering the way they'd bristled at each other last night, their casual air all on the surface.

'Oh, I…challenged something he said.'

'No! Scott, you're not even a qualified doctor yet!'

'Still, I guess I must have hit a sore point or why would he have reacted the way he did?'

'So you actually had an exchange during the lecture?'

'Forget it, Caitlin, it's not important. And he'll be close enough to hear, in a minute.'

'OK...'

To close the subject he rolled her into his arms and gave her a skilful kiss.

Emerging from the salty tangle of his arms and lips a few seconds later, Caitlin was startled to see Angus's gaze fixed upon her with disturbing intensity from beneath his heavy brows. She flinched and stared out at the ocean, her body heat rising to match the hot pressure of the afternoon sun. He shouldn't stare. They'd kissed. They had a right to. They were engaged.

'Thanks for the walk, Erin,' he said.

'No worries,' she answered in a colourless tone. 'I needed the exercise.' She seemed unaware that she was echoing what Angus himself had said.

Then she spread out her towel and lay on her stomach, hiding her face beneath her blonde hair.

Angus saw that Erin had disappeared once more into what were obviously unhappy thoughts, just as she had done on their silent walk. And he had no desire to cramp Caitlin's and Scott's style. Accordingly, he stripped off his T-shirt and turned to the surf with relief. His skin was hot and dry from the walk along the beach, and there was nothing like the buffeting of cold, salty water against your body on a hot day. The afternoon sun reflected white off the foam, and the horizon was a seductive dark blue line.

A strong swimmer, he stroked rhythmically out beyond his depth and then lay back against the undulations of the water. What a pity it was that Rachel couldn't be here! He liked the Grays, liked the contrast of their cheerful chaos with his own quieter and more ordered temperament. But he was beginning to feel distressingly out of place, and he knew that too much of it had to do with Caitlin and Scott.

He hated what he knew about the man, and found himself

wrestling with the issue of Caitlin's rights in the situation. Should he tell her? Or was it none of his business? Scott obviously considered it the sort of dirty little secret that men shared but kept from women. Angus recoiled from that idea…and yet he hardly knew Caitlin. *How* could he tell her something like that? 'I saw your fiancé seducing a twenty-one-year-old med student three weeks ago. Just thought you should know.'

No!

It was possible that Caitlin already knew, he rationalised. Perhaps she and Scott had an 'open' relationship. After all, as he understood it, they hadn't lived in the same city since they'd got involved nearly four years ago. Caitlin had done her nursing training in Canberra, before moving to Sydney.

She didn't seem like the type that would play around. There was a steadiness to her, a maturity…and an innocence, too… And yet what qualified him to conclude all that? Once again, *he hardly knew her*!

The thoughts went round and round in his brain, making it impossible for him to get Caitlin out of his mind as he had resolved last night to do. It should have been easy. *He hardly knew her.* It *would* have been easy, he told himself, if it wasn't for Scott.

As dinner approached, occupied in laying the big table for the adults and the little table for the children, Caitlin found that her thoughts were hovering around the subject of Angus Ferguson in a very annoying manner. Like…like flies around a piece of meat! she concluded crossly. She was almost sorry that he had come down, particularly as his sister wasn't even here, as things had turned out. Perhaps he was regretting it as well. He hadn't smiled in hours.

But the smell of perfectly cooked turkey had an amazing capacity to deflect one's attention from irritating thought-tracks, and only the absence of Rachel cast a shadow.

The Grays were a happy family. No personal tensions exploded across the table to counterpoint the pop of their Christmas crackers, and everyone donned their silly paper hats, examined their silly cracker toys and read out their silly cracker jokes quite cheerfully, especially Scott. He looked absurd and rather dashing in a magenta hat.

Caitlin laughed a lot. Too much. Her face hurt! And she ignored Angus's gaze every time it chanced to fall on her...which seemed to be far too frequently. Had he guessed that her hilarious mood wasn't quite genuine? Did he have any idea why? Because *she* didn't!

What on earth is he thinking? she thought angrily, as she flicked her gaze from his for the fourth time. I *definitely* wish he hadn't come!

He...Angus...was up early on Boxing Day.

So was Caitlin, despite her firm intention of sleeping in. Somehow she'd had a restless night—maybe too much Christmas pudding—and already the sun was bright in the room. For some minutes she pretended to herself that she *wasn't* awake, but finally admitted that she just *was*, and felt she may as well make the best of it. An early walk along the beach in a windproof jacket and bare legs and feet would be glorious.

Angus had obviously thought so, too. She met him as they each came around the house from opposite directions. He must have come out via the balcony, while she'd come out of the downstairs door and walked across the front garden.

Her heart sank. She hadn't wanted to see him! Hadn't wanted to see *anybody*, not even Scott!

Scott had refused to join in games last night. He'd once again tried to get Caitlin to make a change of sleeping arrangements—couldn't all the children be put in together on the floor with sleeping bags or something? And he was miffed because she refused to suggest anything so selfish and difficult. Erin had declined games, too, in favour of sitting alone on the balcony, staring at the ocean.

This left Caitlin paired with Angus in what had turned out to be an endless game of Pictionary. She hadn't enjoyed playing with Angus, having to sit close at his elbow as they'd interpreted each other's sketchy drawings to guess the mystery word. The fact that they'd eventually won was immaterial.

She frowned darkly, thinking back on it, and this was the expression that greeted Angus. He looked similarly disturbed at the sight of her, and didn't trouble to hide the fact, which prompted Caitlin to dispense with any pretext of politeness. 'Which way are *you* going?'

'Uh…'

'Because if it's south, *I'll* go north to the rocks! And vice versa.'

'Actually, why don't you—?'

'No. Please.' She gestured generously at the beach. 'I come down here all the time. You're the one who hasn't explored much so you choose.'

'I was going to say there's no reason why we can't go together,' he said calmly, 'but obviously there is.'

'Yes. That is—'

'You want to commune with nature in solitude,' he finished for her. Like her, he was wearing shorts and a light jacket, and the sea breeze was ruffling his dark hair.

'Yes!' she answered him. 'Uh…thank you for understanding.'

'Thank you for making your desires so plain,' he returned. He had an amazing mouth, incredibly expressive without being over-full. How could just one little tuck at its corner, which wasn't quite a smile, communicate such a mixture of reserve and amusement and…something else, which she didn't attempt to name? 'I'll take south,' he finished.

At this point, of course, she should have left the whole

subject alone and gone on her solitary way. But for some reason she couldn't. 'I suppose you think I'm incredibly rude,' she challenged him, lifting her chin and meeting his steady look without a twitch.

'I could be tactful and call it plain-spoken,' he offered with a drawl and that crooked smile again.

'No, don't be tactful. Be honest. I prefer that.'

'Evidently! Then, yes, you were rude,' he conceded gently. 'But as I prefer honesty, too, we can each go our separate ways along the beach and be grateful for the avoidance of misunderstanding. It would have been far less pleasant to only realise halfway through our walk that you'd have preferred to be alone. And I…have a bit of thinking I'd like to do myself.'

With which he stepped back to usher her ahead of him on the banksia-bordered path with exaggerated gallantry, and thus declared the subject closed.

After all that Caitlin didn't enjoy her walk. For once she was at heart oblivious to the glorious sight of morning sun on the deep blue-green of the water and the silver-gold curtains of spray that regularly misted the air, though she tried to tell herself how beautiful it all was. Nor did she relish, as she usually did, the different textures of cool, squishy sand and rough, flat rock massaging her bare soles.

She spent a full ten minutes trying to forget her annoying exchange with Angus, and a further five minutes planning to be a little annoyed with Scott if he wasn't up by the time she got back. She worried about Rachel and the baby. And finally she put in some very unproductive thought time in trying to calculate at what point she should turn back if she wanted to avoid staring at an approaching Angus for half the journey.

I'll start back now, she finally decided. He's miles away. I'll get to the house way before he does.

Only she hadn't accounted for the fact that he was jogging, and there he was pounding towards her as she approached the path to the house, sending up a sparkling wake of surf from the shallows where he ran every time a fresh wave creamed around his olive-skinned feet.

Deliberately Caitlin slowed down and pretended to examine some shells—actually, they were quite lovely, with insides smoother than glass and the colour of newborn skin so she kept a couple for Scott. This should have allowed Angus to gain the path first and disappear amongst the banksias, but to her absolute frustration he insisted on waiting for her, right where a big, golden cylinder of banksia flower stood to attention above his head like a beacon.

'I've been thinking about our recent conversation,' he said to her, just as pleasantly as before. 'Is honesty a game you like to play by yourself, or can anyone join in?' His dark eyes glinted.

'It's not a game at all,' she retorted, glaring at him.

'Perhaps not. I won't beat about the bush, then. Is everything all right between you and Scott?'

'Fine.' Her gaze flew up to his in alarm. He'd *noticed*? Even Mum hadn't! He was still watching her and she knew he didn't believe her, so she added in a rush, 'Except that he's a bit annoyed at not getting to…have more time alone with me.'

She at once regretted saying so much to a near-stranger and finished, more bluntly than she should have, 'Not that it's any of your business!'

He hesitated. 'No. You're quite right. I apologise.'

'Oh…please… *I* should do that!' she said, repenting. *Why* did she find this man so disturbing? 'The trouble is… Well, I think we're all a bit worried about Rachel, aren't we?'

'There's no need. Really,' he said warmly.

And she felt like a heel when he spent a good four minutes assuring her that Rachel and her baby had every chance of being fine, and explaining exactly what would happen if birth did come early.

'Thanks,' she told him at last, her voice unaccountably husky. 'Thanks, Angus!'

'Any time,' he answered her, and there was an odd light in his eyes that she couldn't read at all. 'It's good to know that you care about my sister.'

And before she could say anything more, he had turned to stride ahead of her to the house.

'Now, as long as Scott is up…' she muttered to herself, starting off after him.

But he wasn't.

'Caitlin's an early riser, too,' she heard Mum say to Angus as she entered the kitchen.

'No, I'm not, Mum!' she protested defensively at once. 'I quite often sleep in till, oh, seven or seven-thirty at least!' It wasn't a very impressive claim.

Mum turned, astonished. Then her eyes narrowed in sudden assessment and she flicked a glance of quick, silent calculation between the two sandy-footed beachcombers. There was an odd moment of slightly embarrassed awareness between all three of them, then Mum broke it with a vague, hearty, 'Well, I'll squeeze a jug of fresh orange juice, shall I?' The dangerous moment passed.

'Here, I'll do it,' Angus promptly volunteered, in his darkly male voice.

Caitlin went to have a shower and stayed there for a long time, washing the salt out of her hair. Hiding. She knew she was hiding, just didn't want to look too closely at why.

CHAPTER THREE

AFTER breakfast had been cleared away, Peter got everyone organised for a picnic to the Mullaby Island rock pools to give Rachel and Gordon a quiet day. Erin chose to stay home as well. They set out at ten-thirty, had a swim and a play on the beach, then ate their picnic and finally went to explore around the pools.

Scott, who hadn't been very interested in Caitlin's shells, was fully prepared after a hearty picnic lunch to be quite enthusiastically interested in rock pool life. The kids thought he was hilariously wonderful as he sprang madly about, doing a wildly overdone imitation of a Scottish marine biologist named Hamish MacCreetur.

'Och, now, here's a wee friend o' mine lairking doon here. We call him the Red Death Anemone, Sean, de ye ken why?'

'No-o!' seven-year-old Sean shrieked ecstatically.

' 'Cos he's de-eathly poisonous, laddie.'

After half an hour of it he was exhausted and visibly bored with the performance, but the kids had got so over-excited by it that they wouldn't leave him alone and he ended up speaking quite sharply to little Anna. 'No, *stop* it! I'm *not* doing the silly voice again, I told you six times already!'

'You didn't have to do it in the first place, Scott,' Caitlin told him quietly, swinging Anna up into her arms for a hug. 'Then you wouldn't have set up their expectations.'

Scott shrugged. 'It's nice to entertain them…but someone else can take a turn now, that's all.'

Which was fair enough. There were plenty of adults to do just that and Scott had certainly done his share, except that the children were confused by the abrupt departure of 'Hamish

45

MacCreetur' and didn't know where they stood now. Did this tall man, who wanted to be called Uncle Scott, like them or not?

Meanwhile, Caitlin couldn't help noticing, Angus Ferguson had hung back a little from the children, gravely answering several of Sean's endless questions and lifting Ashley over a wide crack in the rocks without being asked, but not by any means playing the clown or the charmer. A careful approach to winning them, in other words. Unwillingly, she respected it.

They went right out to the end of the rock shelf where a harder section of sandstone had remained less weathered, providing a barrier against the sea which could be climbed to give a view of glassy blue-green waves swelling and curling and breaking against the tangle of kelp clinging to the knotted stone. It was wonderful to watch the waves and smell the fresh salt spray. Caitlin could have done it for hours, but the children started to clamber too daringly and Anna was badly overdue for her nap.

Scott seemed to be getting restless, too. He started wandering back in the direction of the cars parked behind the sandhills that overlooked the beach, the rock shelf and the low island beyond.

'If we went back by ourselves in your parents' car, would everyone fit in the other three cars?' he said. 'We haven't been alone since we got here.'

She turned to him, hiding the wave of reluctance that suddenly swamped her. She didn't *want* to be alone with him! She didn't like the way he was behaving this Christmas! The strength of the feeling appalled her, and took her totally by surprise.

'No, we haven't,' she agreed, struggling to appear relaxed. 'But as to the cars… No, I don't think we can. With the bulky car seats that Tyler and Anna have, everyone would be a bit squashed.'

Scott shrugged. 'Perhaps we could go out to dinner…' He glanced back at everyone else. 'Just us?' he suggested.

'That'd be nice,' Caitlin agreed. It would! Of course it would!

'Meanwhile,' Scott said next, 'maybe I should resurrect the ould Professor MacCreetur.'

'You don't have to, Scott, really. The children are—'

But he was already off, although there were currently no children anywhere within earshot, exclaiming in his outrageous, high-pitched Scottish brogue, 'What's yon wee devil I see here?'

Unfortunately, although he realised the fact too late, there *was* a devil in the pool he had chosen. Caitlin was right behind him and saw the whole thing, and it happened so fast that it left her winded with shock.

Scott had innocently brushed aside some mustard-yellow seaweed that floated from beneath a rock ledge in order to get a closer look at another lovely anemone. 'Look at this wee white flower of a thing!' he was saying, his hand still pushing the grape-like weed back against the rock, when the water suddenly boiled with movement as a very small tentacled creature, clearly believing itself to be trapped, emerged from beneath the concealing ledge and attached itself to his forearm.

'God!' he snarled, pulling his hand from the water. 'It's a blue-ringed— Bloody hell! Caitlin, it's bitten me! I didn't feel a thing, but I can see the blood coming. *Hell!*' Frantically, he shook the octopus off. It didn't try to keep hold but untied those oozing tentacles and plunged back into the pool, disappearing as quickly as it had come.

Its body was only the size of a walnut and its tentacles each just a few inches long, but Scott was white and panic-stricken, and rightly so. The bite of the blue-ringed octopus could be deadly.

'Oh, hell,' he muttered again through numb lips.

'Don't talk, Scott,' Caitlin urged. 'Calm down. Just lie down while I get—'

Angus. He was just yards away already. One last leap across one of the pools which had seemed so innocent and lovely until a moment ago brought him to where Caitlin and Scott stood. He didn't waste any time.

'It bit you?' Very terse. No warmth.

'Hell, yes!' Scott lay down clumsily on his back and stretched out the injured arm. 'For God's sake, get a pressure bandage on it quickly!'

Caitlin was already pulling her own short sundress over her head. She had her classic black and mauve one-piece swimsuit on under it, but would have removed the dress even if she hadn't. The fabric was strong, however. 'I—I can't get it to rip.' Her fingers felt like jelly.

Angus grabbed it and stretched it across a rough piece of rock then pulled sharply and there came the gratifying sound of cloth tearing. Working fast, he soon reduced the skirt into strips of approximately even width while Caitlin began the best bandage job of her life—a tight, regular, overlapping weave from fingers to elbow.

Someone could have photographed it for a textbook, but she suddenly doubted what she was doing and demanded wildly of Angus, 'Is this a waste of time? Am I taking too long?' Scott was whimpering and moaning. 'Shouldn't we just get him out of here?'

Angus's strength and control drew her like a magnet, and in the middle of the drama she didn't stop to question her response to him.

'It's vital,' he snapped impatiently. He was using a wider span of torn cloth to fashion a sling which would immobilise Scott's arm close to his body.

Although they'd worked efficiently, it had seemed to take for ever. The rest of the group, however, absorbed in child-minding and wave-spotting, had only just seen that something was wrong and were heading this way. The waves drowned out the sound of voices easily so there was probably no point in shouting the story at them yet.

'Get things in perspective,' Angus continued to Caitlin. Why did he look at her that way? She'd never felt such an urgent need to know the substance of another human being's thoughts. 'This buys us untold extra minutes. His body will even begin to break down some of the venom so that it never reaches his heart and lungs.'

'Oh, hell, I hope so!' Scott croaked.

Finished!

'Now we've got to get you to hospital,' Angus said to him, fighting to conceal his dislike. He cared about the man's life. That was too ingrained in him professionally to change with personal feelings, no matter how negative. But he didn't care for the man, and he hated himself for not being able to overlook that even now.

'I know, but—' Scott had raised his head and looked along the rock shelf back the way they had come. What had seemed like a pleasant stroll, well within the capabilities of small children, now looked like a yawning distance, and then, once in the car, there was the rough kilometre of track that led to the main road, followed by several more minutes of highway driving. It wasn't going to be an easy trip.

Meanwhile, the potent neurotoxin in Scott's system could begin to reveal its symptoms within minutes as it inevitably began to escape the restraining web of the bandage.

Angus wasted no time in calculating the odds. He bent his back and heaved Scott into a fireman's carry. 'You've got to relax, mate,' he said, forcing encouragement into his voice. 'It's not going to be easy for you, I know, but don't waste your breath telling me about it because I'll have troubles of my own!'

'Angus, you can't carry him all that way,' Caitlin protested, but he only gave her a brief, speaking glance before starting off, managing an incredible low-slung lope that was almost a run.

Caitlin understood the glance at once, and had to accept what it meant—there was no other choice. Over the rough terrain of the rocks, made maze-like as it was by pools and wide, water-filled crevices where sea water gushed and gurgled, swelled and sank, any sort of carry that involved more than one person would be far too slow and awkward. Also, Scott's position now, draped across Angus's back like a sack of potatoes, offered him the best opportunity of keeping the vital degree of relaxation and stillness that would slow the spread of the toxin through his system.

Caitlin's throat tightened. Scott's life was in danger, and the thought of it was making her limbs shaky. She was certain that any second she was going to fall on the sand and sob helplessly. She was equally certain that if anyone could save him it was Angus Ferguson, who was still maintaining that heroic, incredible pace across the rocks. Why did he dislike Scott so? It was obvious, even now. The issue sapped her strength even further.

But at least she *could* fall on the sand and sob, couldn't she? Her part was over. It was all up to Angus's heroism now.

No! Wrong!

Her nursing training fighting to the fore again, and the issue of what she did or didn't feel for Scott forgotten, she started desperately after them.

'What on earth is going on?' said Caitlin's father, arriving a little breathless beside her at that moment and halting her in her tracks.

Everyone else was converging, too, though no one else had been close enough to see the details of the drama, it now was clear.

Caitlin's voice deserted her. 'Scott… Scott's been bitten,' she finally managed. 'By a blue-ringed octopus. And they're not going to the hospital without me!'

With a second, belated spurt of resolve she began to pick her way across the crusty knobs of rock. The tide was coming in now, and some spots which had been dry an hour ago were now under several inches of moving water. In her eagerness to find short cuts, she twice made bad choices, found herself on sections of painfully rough rock, encrusted with tiny periwinkles, and winced as they pressed sharply into her bare soles.

Angus, in sockless leather athletic shoes, had taken a far better route. He was already on the sand, moving more slowly now as his feet dug into it but still impressively strong. At well over six feet, Scott was the taller of the two men by a couple of inches, but Angus's underlying strength and fitness were now completely apparent. A minute later he had disappeared into the scrub-covered sandhills which concealed the cars beyond.

They won't wait for me. They can't afford to. Yet I've got to catch up, Caitlin thought. There's got to be someone else in the car with them in case he needs mouth to mouth…or heart massage…as Angus drives. Oh, let it not get to that point! Let us get to the hospital before the toxin gets that far! I've *got* to catch up!

She only reached Angus's car as he was spinning it out of the muddy rectangle of dirt that passed for a car park, and if she hadn't yelled blue murder at him he wouldn't have stopped.

He roared off again before she'd even shut the door, and his aside to her was impatient and irritable. 'Look, I know you care about him, but—'

Caitlin didn't mince her words either. 'It's not that. I'm a nurse, remember, and he might need resuscitation before we reach the hospital.'

There was a heavy beat of silence, then he said, 'Right. You're absolutely right. I apologise, Caitlin.' For a scant second his dark gaze bored to her very core, making her catch her breath. 'I had no right to speak to you like that about him.'

After that, of necessity, Angus concentrated only on his driving. Was the road really as rough as this on the way in? He took it fast, and normally Caitlin would have been pleading with him to consider the effect on his suspension, and on her spine. As it was, though…

'Any symptoms yet, Scott?' she made herself ask. He was lying silently across the back seat with his eyes closed and his bandaged arm lying on his chest, as if willing his metabolism to slow down, and he replied as briefly as he could, 'Painful. Tongue…lips thingle…thingling.' Then his eyes drifted open and shut again. 'Vision…funny.'

'Get into the back seat, Caitlin,' Angus ordered. 'Watch his breathing and keep checking his pulse. Scott, just lie there, OK?'

He drove even faster, and when he hit the highway he gunned the car like a drag racer.

'We'll have to start paying you a finder's fee,' joked Dr Mann when she caught sight of Angus ten minutes later. He'd pulled his car straight into the ambulance bay as the English doctor was walking through the door.

It was the last joke, however, that anyone at the hospital made for some hours. The next person to say anything remotely funny was Scott himself—very weakly—at almost midnight that night, after artificial respiration and comprehensive treatment with fluids, morphine and a drug to raise his dangerously lowered blood pressure had allowed him to ride out the life-threatening paralysis until it subsided again.

'Bad luck, Caitlin! You never got to give me that mouth-to-mouth.'

'Don't joke!' she ordered, both stern and shaky, meaning it.

She hadn't left the hospital for nine hours, and had only eaten because Angus had brought in a bread roll and a

Thermos of Mum's turkey, vegetable and barley soup and had almost forced the meal down her throat. If it hadn't tasted so wonderfully nourishing she would have resented his attitude in the matter…and resented even more his tender, coaxing tone.

'You really must eat this, you know. We can't afford to have another invalid on our hands, now, can we? Come on, Caitlin, I promise it's very good…'

As he'd said earlier, in a different context, he had no right to speak that way to her! She didn't like it!

Now fatigue and reaction had set in badly, and she didn't know which way was up.

'Caitlin, you're exhausted,' said that same quiet, steady voice behind her. 'Let me take you home.'

She began to protest automatically, then saw that Scott had his eyes closed and was almost asleep. He didn't need her any more tonight. 'All right. Thank you,' she said to Angus briefly, and then almost fell asleep herself during the ten-minute car journey.

It was embarrassing and disturbing to open her eyes at the sound of the engine dying away and find him watching her with a strangely intent expression etched into his dark face. The man had an unusual depth to his eyes. Looking into them, you could be in no doubt of his intelligence, or his perception. If you wanted to, you could probably drown in such eyes…

'I wasn't asleep,' she said quickly.

'I hoped you were,' was his gentle retort. 'You're still badly worried about him, aren't you?'

'Yes. He's my fiancé. And I feel…this is stupid…to blame!'

'It's natural,' he soothed. 'People do in such situations. But don't twist yourself in knots. You *know* it wasn't your fault.'

'I suppose you're right,' she admitted. 'Everyone thinks that way, don't they?'

'Yes. And it doesn't mean… I don't know how to put this,

Caitlin…' He swore under his breath, then said urgently, 'It doesn't mean you owe him anything, OK? Remember that!'

She didn't understand, and screwed up her face. He touched her gently on the cheek with the back of his forefinger and let it slip half an inch, making the tiny gesture into a caress.

'God, what am I saying?' he whispered, half to himself. 'Am I *saying* it or not?'

'I don't know,' she answered with perfect truth, strangely content suddenly at the way he was taking control, immensely soothed by the simple feel of his tanned fingers on her skin.

'Look,' he said firmly, taking his hand away, 'all you need to realise at this point—' He spoke with some effort—'Is that we got him there in time, OK? There should be no long-term effects at all.'

'Then why are they keeping him in?' she demanded, her widened eyes still fixed on his dark face. 'What about kidney damage?'

'I had a talk with Dr Mann. She said his kidney output was fine. But they do like to play it safe in cases like this. They'll keep him in until Monday morning, and ask him to take things pretty easy for a couple more days after that.'

'Right.' Caitlin nodded, letting her head drop. She was too tired even to take this in properly, too tired to notice that Angus was still watching her carefully, too tired to do anything but walk numbly into the house with Angus quiet at her side, say a few words to Mum and collapse into bed.

It wasn't until she had woken the next morning at nearly ten, after over nine hours' sleep, that the implications of Scott remaining in hospital for another night struck her. With Christmas and Boxing Day over, she was due back in Sydney tonight, ready to start an early shift on 6A Surgical at seven the next morning, and he was supposed to be driving her back.

It emerged over a late breakfast, however, that Mum had it all arranged.

'Angus will take you,' she announced.

'But—'

'He'll have you for company, which will be nicer than driving alone,' Mum said.

'Oh,' said Caitlin, wishing she hadn't slept in. She'd rather catch the bus than spend several hours alone with Rachel's disturbing brother, but she couldn't say that now it was all arranged.

'I understand I'm getting a lift with you,' she told Angus rather stiffly when they first encountered each other a short while later on the balcony.

He hadn't caught the stiffness, fortunately. 'Yes,' His answer was bland. 'And I'd like to leave at three, if you don't mind.'

'Make that a quarter to?' she suggested. She was fighting hard for something but didn't know what it was. 'That way we can stop at the hospital on the way through and I'll say goodbye to Scott.'

'Of course,' he responded easily, and excused himself to disappear inside.

She didn't see him for the rest of the morning. Robert and Sue and Peter and Lisa were taking their children for a hike so they dropped her off at the hospital shortly after ten-thirty in Peter's four-wheel-drive, and she stayed until lunchtime when her father picked her up again.

Scott was feeling much better today and tried to be an entertaining patient, full of jokes and teases and anecdotes, despite Caitlin's protestations that he should relax, so she was quite relieved to see her father. Alone, Scott would get some rest.

Back at the beach house, she had a quick sandwich for lunch and then headed down to the water for a last swim, feeling very strongly that the Christmas break had gone too fast and been too stressful.

There's just been too much drama, she decided, with Scott and Rachel each giving us all such a scare.

Rachel was still taking things very quietly, which didn't help Caitlin to relax. Normally, her bubbly personality would have helped to include Angus and make things run more smoothly.

And Caitlin had to report to her sister-in-law that the latter's hopes regarding Angus and Erin were a lost cause.

'Rachel, she's moping and she just wants to be alone. Maybe in six months when she's settled back into life at Southshore again…'

'Still,' said Rachel, clinging stubbornly to her dream, 'ask him about her in the car if you can, Caitlin. Find out if he made any sort of an impression.'

'If I get the chance…' she promised reluctantly, privately deciding that matchmaking wasn't a hobby she'd be in any hurry to take on.

Deliberately, she stayed in the water until it was time to change and pack. Angus turned up for a surf as well, but the beach was big enough and crowded enough at this time of year for them both to be able to pretend they hadn't seen each other. Promptly at a quarter to three they were seated in his car, with all their goodbyes said.

'Now…to the hospital,' Angus announced as they turned onto the main road.

'Really, though, if you—'

'I told you I was quite happy to stop, and I am,' he said evenly, and she knew it would be annoying of her to press the point.

Accordingly they stopped, and Angus left the car as well to find a magazine to pass the time with in the bright, pleasant waiting area. Unfortunately, though, when Caitlin was ushered in to see him Scott was sound asleep.

'When did he drop off?' she whispered to the nurse.

'About half an hour ago. He tired himself out, flirting with Sister Eames after lunch.'

Caitlin laughed, although she wasn't quite sure that it had been a joke. If he *had* been flirting, he'd evidently quite exhausted himself with the activity. He slept for a further hour and a half. Caitlin, of course, kept insisting to Angus that it didn't matter about seeing Scott awake and they should leave. He kept insisting that, on the contrary, it clearly mattered very much and they were going to stay.

Eventually, the politeness of their respective positions became so stubborn and determined that if they'd been just *slightly* less civilised people Caitlin would have been dragging him bodily in her wake down the corridor towards the exit and he would have been hoisting her, kicking and screaming, into his arms and carrying her back again.

As it was, since they *were* civilised, all that happened was that Caitlin got more and more long-winded in her protestations while Angus became ever more terse and to the point in his.

'Really, I must absolutely *insist* that we leave now because if we don't it'll get to the point where—'

'No, Caitlin.' Very controlled and heavy. 'We'll stay.'

Angus won. Caitlin was beginning to understand that he probably won battles like this a lot.

At five o'clock Scott woke at last. It was an anticlimax. He was feeling so much better after his sleep that he couldn't even summon any regret at parting from her.

'I'm going back to Sydney now, Scott. Angus is driving me, as I told you this morning.'

'That's nice.'

'Look after yourself. Let Mum spoil you rotten after you're discharged.'

'I will.' He stretched luxuriously.

'Phone me when—well, whenever you want to.'

'Of course.'

'Goodbye, then.'

'Bye, babe.'

She bent down and brushed a swift kiss against his lips, absurdly self-conscious in front of Angus who had just appeared in the doorway. Straightening again, though, she found that he hadn't even been watching. He was checking something very studiously in a small diary.

Now he put it away and said gruffly, 'Ready?'

She nodded, touched Scott on the shoulder and left the room.

Angus said nothing as they walked down the corridor together, and she wondered if he was angry at having waited an hour and a half for that brief scene. He seemed to be! Perversely and unfairly, she was angry herself—the way a perfectly normal and well-adjusted person could be angry at someone who had insisted on putting himself out for one's own benefit. She was painfully aware, in other words, that he had forced her into his debt, and she didn't like the fact.

I'd really rather be on the bus! she thought uncomfortably.

'Have you been engaged to Scott for long?' Angus asked.

They were heading up the highway out of Houghton with the open green dairy country all around them. It wasn't the sort of question Caitlin had been expecting. She had planned to stick to the safest of topics—the weather, the scenery and the children's reaction to Christmas—with perhaps one side-trip into whether Angus had enjoyed his stay. She was quite sure he hadn't—perhaps he'd enjoyed Christmas even less than she had—but he probably wouldn't admit it.

'Almost four months,' she answered him, while the back of her mind was buzzing with these thoughts. 'But we've been going out together for nearly four years.'

'Yes, I knew that. It's a long time.'

'Is that a problem?'

'Of course not. I was just wondering if you'd found all the

separation hard.' It sounded like a casual question, but Caitlin had the feeling it wasn't.

'Well, of course,' she answered. 'But I'd already started my nursing course in Canberra when we met—his family's from Canberra—while he was more than two years into his medical studies at Newcastle. But I moved to Sydney as soon as I was finished because that's where he intends to settle, and that brought us a lot closer. We've seen each other as much as we could. I've felt guilty about it sometimes. He hasn't done as well in his studies as he'd hoped, and I'm sure it's because of travelling down to see me.'

'You think that's why he hasn't done as well? Perhaps he just didn't work hard enough!' Was that a joke? It didn't seem to be.

'He worked *very* hard!' She couldn't keep a squeak of indignation from her voice. 'Why are you suggesting that?'

'Just wondered,' he answered mildly. 'Medicine's tough. Some people…get distracted.'

'Well, Scott doesn't!' she claimed, though underneath she knew she was being too generous. There had been a few times when he'd told her he'd be at home, studying, and she'd phoned to find that he hadn't been there at all. 'I needed a break so I went out with some friends.' That had been the usual explanation.

'I'm sorry. I've been too critical,' Angus was saying.

'Yes! Since you hardly know either of us. You don't seem to have much in the way of small talk, I have to say, Angus Ferguson!' Odd, she'd have been less angry if his words had been further from the truth.

He sighed. 'OK. I concede you have some justification for thinking so.' Then he gave a crooked grin. 'Let me try and convince you otherwise, then.' There was a short silence, then he added in a very different tone, 'These coastal forests really are beautiful…'

'Yes, gorgeous.'

'Is that acceptable as small talk?'

'Perfect!'

'Sincere, too. Do you come—? Yes,' he answered the un-completed question himself. 'I remember. You said the other day that you *do* come down here quite often.'

'Several times a year. By myself sometimes, or with a cou-ple of friends. And with Scott. Even in midwinter it's glorious. And so relaxing after the pace of Sydney.'

'Then you'd recommend Cargo Beach, or the Houghton area, as a place to look for real estate now that I'm settled?'

'What, you're looking for a beach house?' She turned to him in surprise, forgetting her annoyance.

He was concentrating on the road ahead as they were wind-ing down the hill into Myrtle Gully and the road was steep and twisting so he didn't look at her as he explained. 'Sydney is so insanely expensive. I've been wondering about just buy-ing a studio and then getting a bigger place out of the city altogether to escape to at weekends.'

'It's a bit far, surely.'

'Probably. I might look north of Wollongong. Coalcliff or somewhere. My plans are very fluid. I'm really not serious about it yet.'

'Right.'

Silence.

'So, you say you're permanently settled in Sydney now?' she questioned brightly after a moment, uncomfortable about the lack of talk. For some reason, as soon as they weren't saying anything she immediately began to feel uncomfortable about what he might be thinking.

'Yes,' he answered. 'I've enjoyed all my travels…learned a lot…been lucky in the professional opportunities I've had, but this position at Southshore is a good one and it's time I gave myself the chance to pursue some other goals—goals that aren't connected with medicine.'

'But tell me more about your travels,' she persisted. If she could keep him to a topic that was geographically distant, maybe she'd feel more physically distant from him too. At the moment she was far too aware of him and this car seemed far too small. She was used to sitting beside Scott.

'Well, New York and Edinburgh are both fascinating cities in their different ways,' he began, and they were approaching the Kiama bypass before she allowed him to draw breath. 'Whew!' He gave her a quizzical glance. 'You can make a man talk, can't you?'

'Oh, no!' she insisted firmly. 'I just asked a few questions, and you did the rest.'

'No,' he insisted in turn. 'I refuse to take the blame. You gave such a convincing performance of being interested—'

'Well, I was…' *Almost* to the point of forgetting to feel uncomfortable with him.

'That you brought it all on yourself. Now…' He slowed and veered to the Kiama exit. 'I need a break so, if you don't mind, we'll stop to eat.'

She did mind, of course, but could hardly say so. The idea had been to get this trip over as quickly as possible. She didn't want to prolong their contact with a friendly meal. But they'd left an hour and a half late, which was entirely her fault, and if he was tired…

They got pizza. For Caitlin it was traditional. If a mealtime and Kiama happened to coincide, she got pizza. Often she ate it as she drove. But Angus had other ideas.

'I've never seen the famous blow-hole,' he said. 'It's a nice afternoon. Let's sit up in the park and see Kiama's best tourist attraction perform. And I fancy a beer. You'll join me, won't you?'

'Why not?' Caitlin agreed weakly. Pizza and beer were one of life's more ideal couplings, but the stuff always went to her head somewhat. Maybe that would be good! She'd relax! He seemed to have done so already, and she was beginning to suspect she might have to revise her opinion of him a little.

What *was* her opinion, though? At the moment she couldn't quite remember. Scott didn't like him, and he didn't like Scott. Should she take her cue from that, and side with her fiancé? Before the two men had met on Friday night, she and Angus had got on perfectly well. Wonderfully well. Dangerously well.

She warned him, hoping to put him off the picnic plan altogether, 'I doubt that the blow-hole will be performing much tonight. The sea's dead flat.'

But he only shrugged. 'I'll see it another time. I'd still like to sit up on the headland.'

'Yes, it would be lovely.'

He'd understated the evening. It was gorgeous. Six o'clock, still warm but not hot, the sea sparkling, the coastal escarpment in the distance lush, and every now and then a small roar and a 'plock' noise, and up would come a spume of spray from the blow-hole at the end of the frayed, jutting headland of bare dark rock, hinting at what the waves could do in a storm. Sitting here on the grass, they'd probably have been drenched by it. She said so.

'It can be dangerous, too, I've heard,' Angus said. 'People washed off the rocks by an unexpected wave.'

'Yes, I wouldn't get too close on a rough day.'

They ate in silence for a while. He had a good appetite, she noticed. They'd ordered an *enormous* pizza with every topping under the sun, and it was disappearing at an impressive rate—as was her beer. Why on earth hadn't she thought to get a light one? Remorse on this issue only led to another large gulp.

Five minutes later the pizza was beginning to taste truly delicious, the whole world was a beautiful place and light beer was a useless invention.

Caitlin finished her meal and lay back on the grass. Angus was still going. He ate with a surprising and very masculine grace as he sprawled on the grass, his weight balanced easily on one elbow and a strong, lean length of leg. No cheese dripped from his chin, and his chewing was silent.

No, not quite. Her perceptions suddenly heightened, she could see his strong jaw working and hear a small, matching rhythmic sound, muffled by the firm closure of his mouth.

He was frowning heavily. Really, he was far too craggy and forbidding to be considered attractive, and his thoughts were obviously as dark as his eyes. What demons haunted the man? she wondered…

Why can't I decide on the right thing to do? Angus asked himself for the hundredth time, scarcely tasting his pizza and immune to the relaxing effect of the beer. Am I normally this vacillating? No!

Then, why?

If he was honest with himself, he knew the answer. It was Caitlin herself. If he hadn't spent that crucial twenty minutes on Friday night thinking that she was Erin… If he didn't, still, feel so powerfully attracted to her… If he didn't think that, at some level, without her even realising it herself, she could very easily be attracted to him…

As it is, all I'm doing is making things worse, he realised. I keep dancing around the subject. She thinks I'm aggressive and unpleasant and rude. She *knows* I don't like Scott! But the very last thing I want is to hurt her, bruise her ideals! That's the problem. That's why I can't say it. I keep trying to find out in advance how she'd react.

And if she would be hurt, badly hurt, I still don't know what would be kinder, more honourable—to *tell* her she's engaged to an unfaithful, two-timing sleaze, or let her keep her innocence as long as she can.

Until it's too late and they're actually married?

He groaned inwardly and, with the issue still unresolved, sprang restlessly to his feet. 'I'm going to look at the blow-hole,' he growled, not meeting her raised eyes. 'Coming?'

Mistake.

She followed him at once, and they stood side by side, leaning over the railing, almost close enough to touch, but not speaking. He could actually feel her warmth, smell the sweet, nutty fragrance of her freshly shampooed hair.

And all of a sudden he just cracked. That was the *only* explanation for the fact that, of all the possible ways to bring up the issue of Scott, he picked the one he did.

He kissed her.

There was nothing gentle about it either. He simply turned her imperiously into his arms and claimed her mouth with his. She gasped and stiffened as if hit by an electric current. He should have stopped right there, but he didn't. Couldn't. It just felt so right to have her in his arms.

She was as lithe and supple and soft as he'd known she would be, and she tasted of beer. It seemed to represent the contrasts in her which he'd responded to so strongly. Beer and shampoo. Yin and yang. The femininity of her beauty, the naturally maternal quality of her relationship with her nieces and nephews, and her feisty side, her tomboy side.

He thought of the way she got up early to go for walks along the beach, and the way she gave as good as she got in the sharp exchanges he'd had with her. He thought of the way she'd bandaged Scott's arm and stayed with him at the hospital for nine hours without thinking once of her own needs, despite the tension he'd seen between the engaged pair over the course of Christmas.

'Caitlin,' he groaned against her mouth, tightening his arms around her.

Would she pull away? She should. Of course she should. She was engaged to another man. That was what this kiss was about, he told himself. He wanted to see how faithful she was.

Not very. She was kissing him back, hungrily, sensuously, with her eyes closed, just as he'd somehow known she would. His fingers came to lift her chin a little so that he could drink in the taste of her more deeply, and when she raked her nails down his back, a gesture of confused violence and need, he shuddered.

Caitlin felt the convulsive movement from him and it set up an echoing vibration that sang over every inch of her own body. She leaned into his chest, feeling her neat, firm breasts crushed against him through the thin cotton knit of her blue and white T-shirt as she brought her arms upwards to wind them hungrily around his neck. Then she heard a little mewing sound which, she realised with distant astonishment, had escaped from her own throat.

He gave a ragged growl of triumph and deepened the kiss still further, until she was gasping and arching her back, thrills chasing each other down every nerve in her spine.

Their kiss lasted until children's voices approaching on the path behind them reminded them that this was a public place. Children, too, were a little too closely connected to family. Her family. Her fiancé…

They both broke away from each other in the same moment, making an effort to control their breathing, and Caitlin said at once in a low, shaky voice, 'I've *never* done that before.'

'What, kissed a man?' he growled. It was a wilful misunderstanding, a deliberate challenge.

They were still standing too close to each other. Closer than they needed to be. He had only muttered the question, but she had heard it quite clearly and almost felt the rumble in his chest.

'No! Betrayed my fiancé!' she retorted, deliberately harsh.

'You didn't betray him. It was only a kiss,' he stated baldly.

'Only? That's a cowardly quibble, Angus, and you know it. That was much more than a kiss.'

He was watching her, his eyes narrowed and assessing, and after a short, thick silence he said abruptly, 'OK, I won't deny that.' Then, challenging her, he said, 'So what are you going to do about it?'

'Do?' she echoed, then gave a mirthless laugh. 'I'm going to break my engagement to Scott, of course.'

The words were out of her mouth before she could fully consider what they meant, and when she heard the echo of them in the air she felt sick.

Had so much changed in just a moment?

Angus didn't seem to think so. 'Why?' he urged harshly. 'For a kiss? Don't you think that's a bit extreme? Scott need never know. We could go to your flat, make love together all night long for the next three days and he need never know. He's hours away. Then you could go on as if nothing had happened. You were young when you got together...'

'I was nineteen,' she confirmed.

'He was your first lover, wasn't he?' He didn't wait for an answer to this. 'Doesn't every modern woman have the right to sow her wild oats? You'll marry him next year with the secret satisfaction of having had your fling. You'll be happy together. Maybe for ten years. Maybe for the rest of your lives. And he need never know...unless this episode gives you a taste for open relationships. Where's your courage, Caitlin? Where's your sense of adventure, and your imagination?'

'Not in the same *universe* as yours!' she hissed. 'I responded to your kiss, yes. I just—It overwhelmed me. I've never felt like that before. So instantly on fire.' It swamped her again. He was still so close she could have run her palms over his chest just by reaching out a few crucial inches.

'Not even with Scott?' he probed.

'No! *Not* with Scott! And I hate myself for it! And if you think there's *any* chance of repeating this, let alone us going to bed together...! But it's taught me something at least. It's made sense of things I'd been feeling for weeks without realising it. I don't love Scott the way I should. If I could respond like that to you then I don't love Scott the way I should, and the only fair, decent thing to do is to admit my mistake and break off our engagement as soon as I can.'

'You look a bit green...'

'Yes! I feel sick! The thought of ending it this way for this reason is... But I don't feel half as sick about that as I'd feel about doing what *you* suggested!'

He looked at her for a long moment, then said steadily, 'Good. I'm very glad you said that, Caitlin.'

'What?'

'I have to confess I was playing a little game. Devil's advocate. You've probably heard of it.'

'When you kissed me?' She felt even sicker, though it shouldn't have mattered whether his kiss had been sincere or not. This whole thing was really nothing to do with Angus. It was her own response that was the problem.

'No! Not then!' he rasped urgently. '*That* was real! I wanted you, Caitlin. I still do. But don't worry. I know it's not going to happen. Not yet anyway.'

'Not *ever*!'

He ignored that. 'But when you talked about ending your engagement, I wanted to find out...'

'Yes?'

'If you really meant it. You've convinced me. You do.'

'Why?'

'Why?'

'Why did you want to know? I know you detest Scott. That's been apparent from the beginning. But why on earth should it matter to you about the state...or status...of our relationship? Are you the type who enjoys messing with other people's feelings?'

'No,' he answered quietly. 'The opposite, I think. I'm the type that *doesn't* enjoy seeing other people's feelings messed with. I don't want to see you hurt, Caitlin. That's all.'

His tone carried such conviction that she couldn't doubt him, although she still didn't understand. Was he really perceptive enough to have realised at once that she and Scott weren't right for each other when, after four years, she'd only just made that still blind, still impossible realisation herself?

She had no response to his words, and felt completely drained. Last night, in the drama over Scott's threatened life, she'd needed Angus and had let herself lean on him. Like the soup he had pressed on her, he soothed her, calmed her, just *helped*. She wanted this help again now.

Help me! If you understand more than you're saying, then tell me! Help me!

She didn't say it. The one thing that she fully understood about her feelings and about what was happening was that she had to handle it alone. It was between herself and Scott. Angus was incidental, and the sooner they were out of each other's company, the better.

As if he'd made the same decision as she had—to get their journey over with—Angus turned away from the railing and strode back to where they'd been sitting. 'Catch that paper napkin,' he called back to her. 'It's about to blow onto someone else's picnic. Then we should get going.'

She hurried after him and did as he'd asked, while he picked up the pizza box and beer bottles and tossed them in the bin. She could barely keep up with him as he walked back to the car, and when they were seated and on the move once again the tension in her coiled body was almost like pain.

Some thirty minutes beyond Kiama they hit the freeway and that helped. Watching the kilometres falling away behind them more rapidly now, Caitlin calculated, 'Only another hour and a half, maybe less, as long as we don't hit traffic.' As it was a quiet day for travel, in contrast to the mass exodus from Sydney on Boxing Day, they reached her small studio flat just two streets from Southshore Hospital in precisely one hour and twenty-seven minutes, as evidenced by his electronic dashboard clock.

'Thanks for the lift,' she gabbled as she heard the boot lock click automatically open behind her. Apart from directing him to the right place, she hadn't spoken for most of the journey. He'd made it just a little easier for both of them by switching on the radio and tuning it to a piece of very full-bodied classical music. It wasn't easy to talk on top of Beethoven.

She opened the door and swivelled to get out, then felt his hand on her arm. *Not* where she wanted it!

'Caitlin?' It was abrupt, urgent.

'Please, let's not rehash—'

'No,' he agreed. 'Not today. Not now. Then let me just say I'm sorry. I chose a bad way of getting my point across.'

'No! Don't try that on me! It was as much my doing as yours, Angus Ferguson, and you know it! You didn't exactly have to work hard to get me in your arms! I don't appreciate it when people try to spare my feelings by whitewashing something I know I've done!'

'Yes, I'm beginning to understand that,' he drawled darkly. 'OK, then, grab your bag and go, please, before either of us manages to create any more opportunities for remorse!'

'Don't even think it!' she snarled, then did just as he'd suggested, pulling her bag from the boot and slamming the lid. He'd driven away into the summer darkness before she even reached the entrance to her building.

Caitlin half expected Scott to phone that night. There was no phone in his hospital room so she couldn't ring him, but he was well enough now to go out to the pay phone in the entrance and make a quick call himself. No phone call came, though, and she was relieved.

I couldn't have a light little chat with him tonight. Not when I know what I have to tell him.

She did, however, ring her parents to report that she'd arrived safely.

'Did you have an interesting journey?' Mum asked.

'Yes.' Very bright. True, too. The journey certainly hadn't been boring.

'That's good, darling. Are you…? I mean, did you like Angus?' Very tentative. Almost a whisper. Caitlin assumed that Rachel was within earshot.

'Yes. Yes, he seems very nice.'

'Nice. Yes.' Mum sounded a little vague now. 'Oh, well, you must get to bed, mustn't you?'

'Better, yes. I start at seven.'

'Bye, then, love.'

'See you whenever.'

It was only after she'd put down the phone that Caitlin realised neither of them had mentioned Scott at all. She was horrified at the oversight, and almost rang straight back, only that surely would have made the glaring omission even more apparent.

CHAPTER FOUR

SOUTHSHORE HOSPITAL at ten to seven on a sunny summer morning just days after Christmas was not the sort of place where a nurse generally found herself fearful of being ambushed from around every corner. Caitlin had certainly never felt that way...

Until today, that was.

This is a large hospital, she reminded herself tightly, as she parked her small motorbike, took off her helmet and headed for the main building. It has over six hundred beds, over fifteen different departments, seven buildings, including a ten-storey main tower, and probably a couple of hundred doctors in and out of the place on a regular basis, not to mention about three thousand-odd other employees.

Angus Ferguson has been working here since the middle of October and we haven't clapped eyes on each other. Or, at least, not close enough to read name-tags. His car park is on the opposite side of the building to mine, and his hours are probably totally different. *We are not going to bump into each other!*

And, indeed, she attained the safety of Ward 6A without the feared ambush occurring...except in her imagination, which managed to play out several difficult encounters in the space of a four-minute walk.

Yesterday—no, the whole of Christmas—now seemed like a bad dream. The only certainty that remained was that she must end her engagement to Scott as soon as she could. The small island of calm in the centre of her being when she thought of this told her it was the right decision, and was

71

echoed by the quiet of the ward as she came in through its open double doors.

With the whole nation poised in the middle of the limbo between Christmas and New Year, very few people were having elective surgery, and every effort had been made in the days leading up to Christmas to get people home to be with their families.

Conversely, of course, it was difficult for the patients who were here to face the fact that they were ill enough to be in hospital over Christmas, and the brightly decorated tree at the nurses' station and festoons of garlands and greenery in the corridor and most of the rooms could not compensate. On the whole, Caitlin liked January better when things began to gear up and there was the sense of getting off to a fresh start.

'Did you have a nice Christmas?' The question, distorted by a huge yawn, came from Ward Sister Josie Wade as the informal shift change conference came to an end at just after seven.

'Sounds like *you* did!' Caitlin retorted cheekily to the older woman.

'Yes! Cooking turkey for twenty then starting work at three so all I got was left-overs. But this yawn…' She did it again. '*Excuse* me! Is for last night. I was late off.'

'You worked all over Christmas? You didn't schedule days off?' Caitlin immediately felt that, as a single, childless woman, *she* should have worked over the break, although she'd taken a turn at that last year and was working New Year's Eve and New Year's Day in a few days' time.

But Josie shook her head. 'I didn't want to. I'm taking the last three weeks of January to go away, remember? And I want to do some of it with accrued days off, not annual leave.'

'That's right.'

'Anyway, things are fairly light today.'

'But last night wasn't?'

'Oh, it was just one patient, really. Betty Reid. She's sched-

uled for this morning, and she was pretty nervous and upset.
She has multiple sclerosis.'

'Surgery for MS?'

'No,' Josie said heavily. 'Surgery for suspected bowel cancer. That's a double whammy, isn't it?'

'And she didn't have anyone with her?'

'Her daughter was here when she was admitted and stayed
for quite a while. Then she had to go off to take part in a
concert or something. She seemed nice. But it was after she
went that Mrs Reid got upset so I stayed late till she went to
sleep.'

'Now, Josie…!'

The ward sister shrugged. 'Sometimes you just have to. I
couldn't simply pat her on the head and say, ''Yes, yes, and
have you finished yet because I want to go home now,
thanks?'' And she seems better this morning. She's due to go
down at ten.'

'Right.' Caitlin nodded, scanning her own list of patients
and finding that Betty Reid was one of them. At the moment
she was in one of the ward's four-bed rooms, but would go
into a private room on her return from surgery later today.

The day's routine was soon fully under way. Mrs Reid was
the only patient going for surgery, but there were several post-
op patients for Caitlin to deal with in varying stages of recovery, ranging from two who were to be discharged that morning
to a road accident casualty who'd come in last night and was
only just out of the recovery suite, following a significant repair to a damaged lung.

Twenty-two-year-old Jason Smart needed his observations
taken straight away. He wasn't a particularly likeable patient,
she soon found—surly, sharp-eyed and ready to complain at
everything—and as his blood alcohol level had been well over
the legal limit last night when he'd been brought in from the
accident, Caitlin had to fight the anger that everyone in the
profession felt in such cases.

Stop complaining! she wanted to tell him bluntly. *And start thanking your lucky stars that no one else was hurt!*

She contented herself instead with the knowledge that the police were planning a more practical approach to the man. As soon as he was well enough they would be interviewing him, at which point he would discover that he no longer had the right to drive.

Next, she stopped at Betty Reid's bedside. The sixty-two-year-old woman wasn't breakfasting today, of course, which made the hours still to pass before she went down for surgery rather long ones. She had a visitor, though. Not the daughter that Josie Wade had mentioned, but a man in his early forties with the sort of face—not particularly handsome—that inspired trust. He stood up to an impressive height as Caitlin approached, and held out his hand at once, saying, 'I'm Julius Marr, Betty's GP.'

He stayed for nearly an hour, by which time the daughter, Stephanie, had arrived as well. A petite, attractive redhead in her late thirties, she was clearly very attached to her mother, and Mrs Reid was evidently the type that rewarded that attachment amply because the two women were soon laughing together and chatting quite cheerfully, to the point where Dr Marr, taking his leave of them, looked almost as if he wished he were part of the family.

Caitlin found herself crossing her fingers extra tightly that Mrs Reid's surgery would reveal only the most minor problem. When she returned from surgery and Recovery late that afternoon, however, the full story was not yet known. A significant mass had been removed, but only follow up tests would reveal its nature and whether there was any spread to other organs or to the bone which had not shown up during surgery. There was a dark, nebulous and ominous suggestion, though, that the mass did not look good and that such a spread was highly likely.

'Not great, is it?' Josie said in a terse aside to Caitlin when they saw the report.

'No…'

Mrs Reid herself was still too groggy to fully take things in, and Caitlin's shift came to an end before Dr McNally had come to see her, which meant a nagging loose end.

Not the best of days, she concluded as she entered the lift on her way home at just after three. But at least she hadn't encountered Angus Ferguson.

Get things in perspective, Caitlin Gray, she scolded herself. You've got a drunken young man who's smashed himself up and a charming older woman who's either dying quickly of cancer or slowly of MS and you're churned up because you can't get one mistaken kiss out of your system!

But she still felt on edge. More so when she got home, and knew that tonight she must phone Scott. He would be convalescing at her parents' house by now. She knew it would be an awful conversation, and it was.

'How are you, Scott?'

'Oh, much better. Your mum's spoiling me.'

'That's great! She's good at that.'

'And I'll be driving up on Wednesday morning.'

'So soon? Please make sure you're—'

'Garbage! I'll be fine. And I have to move, remember?'

He would be living in one of the doctors' residences near Royal Prince Alfred Hospital.

'Of course,' she said thinly. 'Could we meet for lunch on your way through?'

'Yeah, that'd be good. Just a quick one, though. Hospital cafeteria?'

'Could it be somewhere private? A café? I'm not working until three.'

'If you like. Sick of the hospital muck?'

'Something like that,' she agreed miserably.

'I'll meet you in the main foyer at…what?'

'One o'clock?'

'Great! We'll go from there, and you'll get back in time to change for work.'

They chatted a little longer, and she had to be glad that he evidently couldn't detect the lump in her throat or the stilted effort behind her words, even if she was dismayed at his lack of perception.

'Well, I'd better not run up your parents' phone bill by telling you what I want to do to you when I finally get you alone…'

'No. Better not,' she agreed, her stomach churning. 'Bye, Scott. I'll see you—'

But he'd already put down the phone.

Tuesday, with another early shift, was a quiet, uneventful day, both at home and at work. There was quite a bit of coming and going of various doctors around Mrs Reid, but none of them were saying anything definite yet, which never felt like *good* news. She didn't phone Scott that night. She half thought he might phone her, but he didn't.

Wednesday morning dragged, and Caitlin didn't get much done. She felt nervous and miserable, and teetered on the edge of second thoughts. Perhaps what she felt for Scott was just the way love settled with time, and these irritations and gulfs in understanding were inevitable.

But, no! Not at twenty-three! Not after just four years! Underneath, she knew that was right. It was just…difficult.

Except that, in the end, it wasn't. Scott took it almost *too* well.

'The engagement business was mainly for your parents' benefit, wasn't it?' he said easily. 'It might have been years before we actually tied the knot. If ever! Have you met someone else?'

'No!'

He shrugged. 'OK. Just wondered. It's been nice, Caitlin.'

'Nice…' she echoed. She had no right to be disappointed

when *she* was the one to break it off, but he was acting as if she'd cancelled dinner together, not the rest of their future. And he was saying straight out that their engagement had been convenient, expedient, rather than a genuine commitment to share their future lives. That told her, as perhaps nothing else could have done, how fundamentally at odds they had come to be. She was old-fashioned enough to believe that an engagement *meant* something!

'But, Caitlin…' he said after a moment, with his heart-stopping smile. The smile that didn't do a thing for her anymore, she realised. 'I really appreciate that you had the courage to say it first. What we have…just isn't enough, is it? The heat, the sizzle—it's gone.'

'Yes, but don't give me any credit for courage,' she pleaded, her face flaming as she thought of Angus.

He was the one who had forced the issue. Had she thanked him? Probably not. She'd been far too emotional to think of gratitude! And how did you find the words? 'Thanks for kissing my eyes open…'? It didn't work.

She and Scott spent another half-hour talking about plans and practicalities. She had his stereo at her place. He had half a suitcase of her weekend clothes. There were various people they'd each have to tell.

It was like a watered-down, amicable sort of divorce. At the end of it she returned his ring and they kissed briefly, sadly and without passion.

I'm alone. Free, Caitlin thought as she changed into her uniform at the hospital. It felt right, but it didn't feel like something to celebrate. Somehow she had the idea that Scott would be the one to go out partying tonight…

At three o'clock she began work, at three-thirty she handled one of the day's two new admissions and at four, totally without warning, Angus Ferguson walked into the ward.

I am not going to tie myself in knots about this! Caitlin

vowed, as every nerve-ending tingled with powerful awareness and her breathing immediately felt tight.

He looked so different now in his role as a doctor from how she knew him as Rachel's elder brother. Gone were the casual beach clothes and in their place some dark pants, a white shirt and a subtly patterned silk tie, emphasising everything about his uncompromising physique which had overwhelmed her three days ago.

She was at the nurses' station and had been filing the other new patient's chart, making notes about Jason and looking at the stark facts recorded now in Mrs Reid's file. The tumour *was* aggressive, it was fast-growing, it *had* metastasised into other parts of the abdomen and into the bone, where further surgery was obviously not possible, and it was unlikely she would live more than a few weeks longer. The symptoms of her MS had masked the new condition for so long that further treatment—other than palliative care—was no longer any use.

Dr Marr must be feeling *terrible*, Caitlin was thinking, Only it's not his fault at all!

And at that moment, there he was.

No, *not* nice, concerned Dr Marr, but terrible, dangerous Dr Ferguson.

I am *really* not going to tie myself in knots about this!

She didn't have to. He did it for her. She was feeling rather churned up over Mrs Reid, not to mention lunch with Scott, and evidently it showed because he came over at once to say, without the slightest preamble, 'Are you all right, Caitlin?'

He touched her arm briefly across the high desk, but even that airy brush of contact was enough to throw her off balance, set her pulses galloping. She hoped fervently that he hadn't noticed. She didn't want him to lay siege to her, attempt to break down her defences.

'I'm fine. Just a patient, that's all.'

'*Just* a patient?' he queried, a little critically, it seemed to Caitlin.

She retorted far too honestly, 'Well, it's not *yours*, if that's what you were implying.'

'It wasn't.' His response was mild.

She coloured, realising that was not the way she should have spoken to him, then stared down and muttered, 'Oh, Lordy-loo!'

'I beg your pardon?'

'Nothing.'

'Which patient, then?'

'Sorry?'

'Which patient is it that you're concerned about? You look…quite upset.'

The fact that he was still pushing the point annoyed her. Why couldn't he have tactfully vanished under cover of her camouflaging embarrassment? She was *not* in the market for this—whatever 'this' was!

'Um…' she said helplessly. 'Well, it's a Mrs Reid, who's—'

'OK. Never mind.'

'What?'

'I just thought it might have been mine, that's all.'

'I already told you it wasn't yours. I mean, you're a pae-diatric— What on earth are you doing here, anyway? This is an adult surgical ward!' *My* adult surgical ward, said her tone. My territory, in other words, and you're trespassing on it, and I don't want you here!

Her brows knitted together in sudden accusation and her cheeks were still aflame. He hadn't come to see *her*, evidently. The fact should have taken any shred of danger out of the situation, but somehow it didn't. Under the circumstances, if he'd come on other business—and clearly he had—then he should have got on with it straight away and completely ig-nored her—as she'd have done to him if she'd been alert enough to spot him coming!

Now he leaned over the rather high bench top that separated

them. If he'd noticed her somewhat belligerent manner, then he was ignoring it. 'Perhaps she's not here yet. Can I—?' He was trying to see the papers on the desk in front of her, looking for a chart, or something.

'Dr Ferguson, tell me who it is you're enquiring about and I'll find the information for you,' she said in her best nurse-to-doctor voice, polite—deferential even—but totally firm and competent.

'Sure, but I suspect…'

He glanced back to the entrance, 'Ah, here she is!' Sure enough, here was a woman of about his own age, dark and pretty but pale-skinned and obviously emotional.

'Oh, Dr Ferguson!' she said at once, clearly relieved to see him.

'How is he?' Angus demanded, concerned. 'I was down there just before lunch, but—'

'Oh, not good… I can't wait till this is over! If we could do it *now*, this minute, I'd feel—'

'Take it easy, Elise,' he soothed, laying a hand warmly on her shoulder.

Caitlin was immediately shot through with a hot disapproval. My God, the man came on strong with women! For the first time it occurred to her, Perhaps he was just spinning me a line on Sunday, hoping to get lucky on the rebound. Women are notoriously vulnerable then. The 'Devil's advocate' bit was just damage control. After all, he's thirty-five and not married. That starts to look like he doesn't *want* to get serious about a woman. But surely, when he's Rachel's brother…

Then the name 'Elise' rang a bell and she looked down at her list. Elise Best, divorced, aged thirty-five, pre-op. Due for surgery tomorrow to remove a kidney for transplant into her son William, aged eleven.

What is wrong with me these days? Caitlin asked herself.

To object to him touching her when it's obviously what she needed. To read so much into it!

And already Angus's hand had dropped and he was explaining carefully, totally focused on Elise Best, 'We need to get you checked in and finish your work-up.'

'But I thought—'

'Yes, you've already had umpteen tests for compatibility and general health and everything else under the sun when we first began to plan this, but we need to make sure that nothing's changed since. What if you had an infection brewing, or something?'

'I'm sorry, I—'

'I know. You couldn't stand it if something stopped the transplant from going ahead at this stage.'

'Not when you've been telling me since Monday that you didn't think he should wait until our original date, no!'

He spread his hands, 'Elise, all I can say is it's highly unlikely that anything will stop it. Meanwhile, as you're being checked in I'll go down to William and see how he's doing since today's dialysis. We need to make absolutely sure he's ready to go as well.'

'I *hate* this! Of all the waiting we've done over the past few years, this is the worst, I think!'

'But the shortest.'

'Yes, the shortest, I'll give it that,' she agreed shakily.

'Sister Gray...' Angus turned to her at last.

'Yes, Dr Ferguson?'

'This is Mrs Best. I think you'll have gathered—'

There was a definite degree of reproach in his dark look. 'Yes,' she cut in quickly. 'We've been expecting you, Mrs Best.'

'I'll come back up after I've seen William, Elise,' Angus said. He touched her briefly on the shoulder again and left the unit.

'Come this way.' Caitlin turned to the jittery mother. 'I'm

afraid we'll have to ask you all sorts of questions that you've answered about a dozen times already.'

'That's all right.' Elise Best smiled faintly. 'Probably best if I keep busy!'

'It'll all be over this time tomorrow.'

Caitlin had said it to so many patients, and very often it was all she could say, although she knew that its truth probably didn't have much power to help. With some things in life, all you could do was wait out the hours. After taking full observations, drawing blood and obtaining a urine sample, Caitlin could only leave Mrs Best to do just that.

'So, you see, I do have a legitimate reason for being on this ward occasionally,' Angus said to Caitlin half an hour later, his tone openly and wickedly triumphant.

Her head flew up and she gazed at him in horror. 'I—' Once again he had attacked her exposed right flank when she'd been off her guard, bent busily over papers at the nurses' station.

'No, you didn't *actually* accuse me of trespassing,' he agreed, grinning. 'But your look filled in any gaps in your sentences.'

Well, she'd said to him the other day on the beach that she liked the direct approach, hadn't she? Since then he'd certainly taken her at her word. They'd practically bared their souls to each other, and she felt that she knew him far better than she wanted to.

She sighed. 'I only meant—'

'Any chance I could grab a coffee?'

'I *meant*—' she persisted.

'OK,' he conceded, opening his hand. It was an apology of sorts, and an invitation to finish her statement.

'That in view of…well, you know…'

'Yes, I know.' He was being very patient. 'Sunday.'

'It would seem better if we at least let each other know if we're in danger of running into each other.'

'Do you think so?'

'Yes!'

'Don't you think that gives the whole episode a degree of importance that you've said you'd prefer to deny?' he suggested gently.

'It wasn't important at all,' she put in crossly.

'Quite! So surely it ought to be business as usual?' His tone was silky, and there was a deep gleam in his eye.

And what could Caitlin do but give a grudging assent? 'I've never seen you up here before,' she accused next, changing tack a little.

He was right, of course, in everything he'd said, but she didn't like his attitude. So typically honest, so…so…*direct*! Yes, she now understood, there was definitely such a thing as being *too* direct.

'No,' he answered her. 'As I said, it doesn't happen all that often. If you like, I'll give you written notice next time.'

'Next time you're here to see Mrs Best?'

'No. That you can now anticipate, I'd have thought. I'll see her post-op a couple of times, although it's Dr Archibald who's doing her surgery. I mean, next time there's a patient here that I'm connected with.'

'Right,' she nodded, then clarified irritably, 'But, *no*! I certainly don't want written notice! How…how ridiculous!'

'I agree. So, are we all sorted out, then?'

'Apparently.'

'Good. Will you now tell me if there's coffee on call in this establishment of yours?'

'I'll make it for you myself if you like,' she retorted, thinking that she'd prefer that to having him fussing about in the sanctuary of the small ward kitchen.

'I was hoping you'd say that,' he drawled unsmilingly, and settled down with the phone. 'Dr Meyer, please,' she heard him say a few seconds later.

Caitlin made him the coffee as quickly as she could—strong and milky and piping hot from an extra zap in the microwave—then put it on the desk in front of him and went about her business without even waiting for a thank-you. He was still on the phone, which made that easier. She spent some minutes with patients—checking Jason Smart's wound, giving Mrs Reid a lesson on self-medication, which it was hoped would combat her rapidly increasing pain, and answering a question from Mr Guarino, her other pre-op admission—and when she next passed the nurses' station Angus was no longer in evidence.

Neither was he in the dining room at seven when she went off for her break. Good!

By nine o'clock the ward was pretty quiet. No more patients returning from surgery or other procedures. No diet maids wheeling dinner trolleys. Mrs Best had been down to sit with her son for as long as she could, which had upset her again, as he was scared about the surgery, but her tests had come back with the hoped-for results so the transplant was definitely going ahead. The degree of compatibility was extremely good, too.

'So do try to get a good night if you possibly can, Mrs Best,' Caitlin suggested gently.

'Oh…' The other woman flapped agitated hands. 'I'll read for a bit to take my mind off it. I keep remembering what you said—"This time tomorrow…" And this time in twelve hours, I'll be under anaesthesia, thank God!'

Oh, those slow, ticking minutes. For Betty Reid the time was dragging too, drawn out by pain that couldn't be fully masked by the narcotic drugs she was now on. She must have been in considerable pain before the surgery as well so she was evidently a stoic. If only she hadn't ignored that warning sign! If only she'd told Dr Marr!

Her daughter Stephanie was still there at half past nine, and now Dr Marr had turned up to give her a lift home, which was nice of him. He looked tired and racked, though, his long, lean body held stiffly and a papery look around his eyes which bespoke a huge headache.

'Busy day?' Caitlin asked gently when he stopped at the nurses' station and asked if Stephanie Reid was still there.

'Pretty busy,' he agreed, with a wide but weary smile, then he dropped his voice to ask, 'Before I go in, how is she taking it?'

'She hasn't said much about that. She seems mainly concerned with the practicalities.'

'That fits.' The doctor nodded. 'She's extraordinarily good at looking after Betty.'

'Oh!' Caitlin exclaimed. 'You're talking about the daughter? About how Stephanie's taking it? I assumed you meant—'

'Sorry.' Julius Marr gave that wide smile again, wry this time. 'I was unclear. Yes, I meant Stephanie. I have an idea I know how Betty views this. But Stevie's the one who has to go on living.'

'Would you like something for your headache, Dr Marr?'

'What? Oh! No, I'll take something later when I get home. But thanks.'

He frowned and headed in the direction of Mrs Reid's room, without remembering to say goodbye, and Caitlin instinctively filed away in her mind the things she had just learned. The family GP was more worried about the patient's daughter than about the patient. Stephanie was called Stevie, and was 'extraordinarily good' as a nurse to her mother.

'Stevie' fitted as a nickname. She came past several minutes later at Dr Marr's side, wearing her russet hair up in a ponytail and sporting a fringed white Western shirt and serious jeans—lots of stitching and studs. Beside the tall doctor she seemed tiny, and he was actually having to bend to hear what she said. Not that he looked as if he minded about that… Stevie Reid was a very attractive woman.

I'll look in on Mrs Reid pretty soon, Caitlin decided. Things can look black for people once their visitors go.

And, indeed, when she went in to the single-bed room half an hour later she found Betty Reid staring at the ceiling with silent tears rolling down her cheeks.

'It's hard,' Caitlin managed. The inadequate words echoed in her ears. The thing was, there *were* no adequate ones.

Mrs Reid struggled to sit up a little higher, then used the automatic button which raised the head of the bed. 'No,' she said firmly. 'I'm not feeling sorry for myself. I'm happy, actually... Only happiness like this comes full circle with grief, I sometimes think. This is what I've prayed for, you see. For Stevie's sake. That at some point I should go quickly and save her life for something better.'

'And yet I'm sure she doesn't resent—'

'Oh, I know she doesn't,' Betty Reid said eagerly. Her speech rhythms were odd—staccato and quavery. It was a multiple sclerosis symptom that many sufferers developed as time went on. Some of her sounds were clumsy, too. 'If she *did* resent it...' she laughed '...I'd probably turn into a witch and want to hang on for as long as I could.'

'Hey, I don't believe that...'

'No, it was the willingness of her sacrifice. She's...such a good person. She needs...more people to be good *to*. Not just me. A husband and children, and now it's probably too late. She's thirty-nine. That rotten fiancé of hers...'

'She's engaged?'

'Oh, not now. No, it was years ago. Before *this*.' Her gesture took in her body, with its advancing MS symptoms. 'But he couldn't take it—that she wanted to look after me. So she had to choose. And she chose me. Didn't tell me either, for months, that was what she'd done.'

So there was divorced Elise Best, ready to donate a healthy kidney to her critically ill child, and widowed Betty Reid, almost embracing her own end for the sake of her daughter's future life. During the shift change-over later that night, Caitlin announced to the night staff of three, 'We have two heroines tonight, ladies.' Then she filled them in on the status of the two mothers.

Then, instead of heading straight off when Carol, Marcella and Bridget took over, she made one last tour of the ward and saw that both women were now peacefully asleep. So was Jason Smart. 'If heroism is catching,' she told him under her breath, standing in the open doorway of his two-bed room, 'you should come out of here just a little bit nicer, mate.'

When the lift stopped to pick her up on its journey down from the theatre suites on the eighth floor, Angus was there, of all people, already on his way out the door as it sighed back. He stopped at the sight of Caitlin, halting her in her tracks, and demanded, 'Are you all right?' That was the second time he'd used that conversational opener with her today.

'Do I really look that terrible?' she retorted indignantly.

'No, not—'

'Because you certainly seem to enjoy telling me so!' The way she enjoyed snapping at him. Or perhaps 'enjoyed' wasn't quite the right word… But it released something somehow. A coiled, painful tension inside her. 'The other day you said I looked green,' she finished accusingly.

'You did,' he asserted calmly. 'And you had every reason to.'

'Well, I hope my feelings aren't showing at the moment.'

'Perhaps I'm just a very perceptive person,' was his drawled reply. It sounded like a mild joke but she was too tense in his presence to smile. 'Is Elise still awake? Or is she down with William?'

'She's here, but she's asleep.'

'And is that asleep as of half an hour ago, or…?'

'It's asleep as of half a minute ago. She was the second-last person I laid eyes on before I left.'

'And who was the last?' he enquired absently.

'Jason Smart. Not someone you want to know about.'

She knew he must have just come from emergency surgery

on a young car-accident victim aged just four years. Here on 6A, they'd had Theatre on the phone to them an hour ago asking about putting the child's father here, but in the end he'd been taken to the ICU. The driver of the other car had been drunk…and completely unhurt.

Perhaps Angus had been asking if *she* was all right because *he* felt wrung out. He said, passing a hand across his face to massage his temples, 'So she's asleep? Good. I won't go in, then.'

The lift doors began to close and he flung out a long arm to press them back just in time. Caitlin stepped in ahead of him with a rather graceless, 'Thanks.' A moment later they were enclosed together. She stood as far from him as she decently could.

Yet, oddly, the emotional connection was stronger between them than the physical one tonight, and that didn't feel unpleasant, perhaps because she knew that his day must have been as challenging as her own.

'How is your patient?' she found herself asking.

He gave a grim laugh. 'Which one?'

'The one you've just put back together, I was thinking of.'

'Oh, you know about that? Yes, I guess you would.'

'We were ready to take his dad, but—'

'Intensive Care got him instead?' he surmised correctly. 'The little guy's not so badly off—now. But only because we got to him quickly.'

'Do you sleep at night after surgery this late?' A vivid picture sprang into her mind of him sprawled on a couch in front of late-night television, with his shirt buttons undone and dark stubble starting to show on his jaw. Then she saw herself in the picture, too, soothing away the strain in his face with her fingers. She snapped the image off like a light, horrified.

'Mostly,' he answered her. 'It's part of the training, you know. Practical Sleep Strategies, Advanced Level. You pass the course when you can drop off like a horse—in a standing position.'

Caitlin laughed. It felt great after the difficult day. Angus was grinning, too. It made him look much more like Rachel, yet at the same time utterly male.

'Occasionally I can't,' he added more thoughtfully, his face settling again. 'If there's anything I think, in hindsight, that I could have done better.'

They left the lift together, and Caitlin dismayed herself by saying, 'Then I imagine your bad nights must be pretty rare.' The last thing she wanted was to respond to him!

'Hey!' He told the empty foyer. 'She's said something nice!'

But this time Caitlin didn't laugh. 'Don't,' she warned.

'Don't what?'

'Don't act as if—' She stopped abruptly.

'As if…?' he prompted patiently.

'We're friends,' she finished lamely.

'But we are, aren't we?'

'As much as we're ever going to be, Angus.' Her tone was made harsh by the sudden tightness in her throat. 'We've been through this. I don't bed-hop.'

'Have I asked you to?'

'You didn't use that term.'

'Because it's not what I was asking from you. Not seriously. You know that.'

'What are you asking for, then?'

'I—don't know. Not this hostility. It's not necessary, Caitlin. I'm not a threat to you. Not to your well-being or your peace of mind.'

Oh, but you are! she thought. Only if I tell you that… Instead, she blurted aloud, 'I broke off my engagement to Scott today.'

'And how did that go?' he asked mildly, not breaking his stride.

'He agreed it was for the best. We've both been…coasting for a while, I guess.'

'You sound sad.'

'I'm certainly not celebrating! Of course it's sad. Endings always are.'

'Even when they're right?'

'Even when they're right,' she agreed.

'I guess I can understand that,' he answered. 'And I respect it, too. You're…an *honourable* person, aren't you, Caitlin?'

'I try to be!'

'More people should.'

'Most people do, don't they?'

'Perhaps.' It didn't sound sincere. 'I'll see you around, then,' he finished casually, then he peeled off down the opposite corridor in the direction of the doctor's car park.

Resisting the temptation to watch him, Caitlin turned in the opposite direction.

CHAPTER FIVE

CAITLIN sometimes considered that New Year's Eve was a harder night to work through than Christmas. At Christmas everyone on the ward was concerned with family and home-style celebration, and making sure that no one felt left out. New Year, though, was a more worldly, sophisticated affair, and in Sydney if you weren't going to a glamorous party—preferably on a private yacht on the harbour with its own live band and the latest in fashionable cuisine—then you weren't going anywhere.

She had been on the harbour last year with Scott. She'd eaten barramundi steak in lime and coriander butter, and avocado-chocolate ganache. She'd danced to live reggae. She'd seen the fireworks cascading over the Opera House and the Harbour Bridge. They'd had a great time. Pretty wild. This year, if she went anywhere, she'd be going alone. The prospect didn't hold much appeal. Probably most people had something much better to look forward to.

In each of the staff members working 6A tonight, there was this same twinge of suspicion that everyone else at the hospital must be out enjoying themselves, 'But not *us*,' Laurel Thompson, heading the team tonight, put it with a laugh.

'We're off at eleven,' pointed out Brooke Peters. 'I'm going to get to *some* party *some*how by midnight if I have to gate-crash a Potts Point mansion to do it!'

Caitlin had no such plan. She'd been invited to a party but had almost decided not to go. It was miles away in Sylvania and without Scott she'd have to get there alone on her little motorbike at eleven-thirty in the evening on the craziest driving night of the year. Then, when she got there, people would ask about him and she'd have to break the news. She hadn't even told Mum and Dad yet.

I'll ring them tomorrow, she vowed to herself. Did that count as a New Year resolution?

'Elise Best is back from Recovery,' reported Josie Wade, who was just going off. 'Betty Reid isn't any better, and her pain management is getting to be a problem. Still nil by mouth. Jason Smart has an infection. Not serious, but serious enough.'

Nobody said anything, but everyone was thinking the same thing. This means we'll have to put up with him for longer.

'Dr Ferguson,' Josie went on, 'phoned twenty minutes ago to say he'd be here in five minutes, so we should probably expect him in about half an hour.' She said it quite seriously and nobody laughed because this sort of thing happened all the time.

'Dr Ferguson?' queried Brooke, however.

'You probably haven't met him. He did the transplant on Elise Best's son. He's pretty new. Started about September.'

'October,' Caitlin corrected unthinkingly. Everyone looked at her. She explained, 'He's…um…my sister-in-law's brother.'

I shouldn't have said that. The last thing I want is to strengthen the connection between us, make it public.

'Really?' Brooke exclaimed curiously. 'So you know him personally?'

'Not very well,' Caitlin answered faintly, wishing she'd said nothing in the first place, just as Angus himself walked through the door.

'Excuse me, my beeper's just gone off,' he said to the assembled nurses, although his glance flicked most directly to Caitlin. He leaned over the desk and grabbed the nearest phone. 'Yes, it's Angus Ferguson here…' he began.

Brooke leaned sideways to Caitlin. 'What a useful sister-in-law you have!'

'What, because—?'

'Because he's *cute*.'

'Do you think so?'

'Don't you?'

'No, actually, I don't think he's very good-looking at all,' she answered truthfully. Not in the way Scott was, so golden and smooth and confident. Her body clamoured at the sight of Angus all the same.

She felt terribly uncomfortable. Why were those shoulders of his so square, and why was that stride so long and confident? You could scarcely ignore his entrance. Her heart was thumping like a sledgehammer.

'You *don't*?' Brooke was squeaking in disbelief.

'Well, no.' She enumerated Angus's weak points with admirable fluency, counting them off on her fingers. 'I mean, his nose has a bump. His eyes are too dark. From some angles his face looks as if it was cut with a blunt axe. And altogether he's just much too…too…'

'Forbidding,' Brooke agreed at once. 'Forbidding is great!'

'Oh, Brooke?' sang out Josie. 'If we could focus, please?'

'Damn!'

The expletive from Angus startled them all for a moment, but he was still speaking into the phone so Josie continued, 'Not much else. It's all on the charts or in the computer.'

'I'll be straight up,' Angus was saying in the background. He put down the phone and turned to Josie, who thumbed his attention across to Laurel. 'Right.' He nodded. 'Look, I was here to see Mrs Best, but there are two children on their way in, quite badly injured after an accident on the Princes Highway. I'll have to get back to her later. Can you tell her…?'

'Caitlin?' Laurel turned to her, and so did Angus.

'Tell her William's doing beautifully. No problems at all. Couldn't have gone better, and I'll talk to her in more detail as soon as I can.'

'She'll be so happy.'

'I know.' He had his hand on the swing door almost before the words were out.

Punctuating his exit, there came the squeal of brakes and the desperate blaring of a horn from somewhere in the streets beyond the hospital. Everyone winced and held their breath, but there was no ensuing crash. Instead, the keening of sirens flared and died, then flared again as what sounded like at least two ambulances pulled into the bay outside A and E on the ground floor.

Now I remember what I *really* hate about working New Year's Eve, Caitlin thought. Waiting for the emergency admissions, and it's still only three o'clock in the afternoon!

Halfway through Caitlin's shift Angus still hadn't made it back to see Mrs Best after Caitlin's interim report to her, but at seven o'clock Ward 6A got its emergency admission.

'Let's hope it's the only one!' Laurel said loudly what they all felt.

Fotini Lyristakis was the mother of the two children who must still be undergoing surgery with Angus. Her own injuries had been severe enough, including a punctured bladder and fractured femur and pelvis.

'But I just pray that the kids are OK,' Brooke said, the light mood she'd been in during shift change quite gone now.

With the new admission, Laurel had shuffled the workload a little to give Jason and several other recovering patients to the younger nurse, while Caitlin kept her current pair of heroic mothers and acquired a third—Mrs Lyristakis. She would be in for some days while the surgery to repair her bladder healed, and then she would be discharged or moved to the orthopaedic ward in the next building if her orthopaedic surgeon considered a longer stay to be necessary. Her pelvis was immobilised as much as possible and her femur was pinned together with state-of-the-art equipment.

'To be honest,' Brooke added, 'I'm glad it's you and not me, Caitlin. She's going to be desperate to know how they are…and what is that going to do to her recovery? Especially if—'

'I can't think about that yet,' Caitlin answered, more firmly than she felt. 'I just have to do the nursing.'

'Who did her bladder repair?'

Caitlin looked at the new chart, which already contained too many pages of notes and forms, all scribbled on in medical shorthand. 'Hunterdon,' she answered. 'But I expect we'll get his registrar…unfortunately.'

The surgeon's registrar, Greg Snow, turned up half an hour later, hard on the heels of his counterpart in orthopaedics. Caitlin still hadn't been off for her break, but hunger was a very distant concern. She was eager to hear if there was any news on Mrs Lyristakis's children, but was disappointed to see Greg, who only had three approaches to any nurse in his orbit. He'd either yell at them, ignore them completely or assume they found him wildly attractive.

'Hi,' he said to Caitlin through his over-full lips, and pinched her on the bottom. 'She's yours?'

'Yes.' Caitlin nodded, gritting her teeth. She knew from experience that the worst thing was to give him a reaction.

'All settled?' he asked, leaning far too close to her with the question.

'Not really awake yet.' She moved away.

'Best for her,' he answered. 'Otherwise she'd be hurting pretty badly. What do you think of her hardware, Nurse? It looks like some hard-core S and M equipment, doesn't it? Is that your scene?'

'I'm sorry. I don't follow,' Caitlin said deliberately, looking as stolid and wooden as she could. 'I don't know much about orthopaedics.'

She wasn't going to let Dr Snow get away with his repellent innuendo. Scott always insisted that flirting was harmless.

When confronted by men like Greg, she didn't agree, but at least she was sure Scott had never come on to a woman as heavy-handedly as this!

It doesn't matter now, she realised almost with surprise. We're not together…

Much to her relief, Dr Snow gave up, for the moment at least. 'I meant the pins in her thighs,' he said with exaggerated patience.

'I understand now, Doctor.'

They both looked at the dark-haired woman. She was about forty-five, short but solidly built, as Greek as her name, with black lashes smudged against her grey-pale cheeks. Normally her skin would be a smooth, well-preserved and very attractive olive, but now her pallor was very perceptible.

'How are the children, have you heard?' Caitlin asked Dr Snow.

'Still in surgery, that's all I know,' he answered. 'One in Theatre One and the other in Theatre Two, with Angus Ferguson shuttling between them and three more surgeons involved, not to mention their underlings. Talk about teamwork! Speaking of which, that's another scene you might be into—'

'How old are they?' she cut across him, sidling quickly round to the other side of the bed to fiddle with some equipment.

'Ten and twelve, I think.'

'And was there anyone else involved?' Just keep the questions coming!

'Another driver. *Not* drunk, apparently, but taking a stupid short cut down a side street to beat New Year traffic and going way too fast. He got off comparatively lightly. One leg broken in four places and no other injuries so Sixth Floor won't see him—he's across in Orthopods.'

'I hope they keep him separate from Mrs Lyristakis if she gets sent over there!'

'It'll be noted, I'm sure,' Greg said. 'Meanwhile, Vasilios

Lyristakis has been contacted, but he's in Newcastle. He's driving down. I expect he'll be here soon.'

He picked up Mrs Lyristakis's chart and scanned the notes that Caitlin had added, and she could only hope that he really had got the message this time.

Things were looking as expected at this stage with the patient. There was some discharge from the freshly sutured wound and it would have to be checked and re-dressed carefully. The nurses in the recovery suite had already ascertained that there were no complications following her general anaesthesia, and her bowel sounds had returned as they should.

Mrs Lyristakis stirred, and Dr Snow scribbled down a couple more instructions. 'We're still waiting for the results on her urine test,' he said.

'For infection?'

'Yes. Won't be in till tomorrow. I'll look for it on the computer and write her up for antibiotics if they're needed.'

'OK. Thanks, Doctor.'

'Meanwhile, later tonight…' He didn't finish the sentence, just left it hanging suggestively in the air and departed, flicking a lock of his dark hair from his forehead with an arrogant toss.

He'd never been nearly so persistent before, and Caitlin knew from experience that he probably didn't remember her identity from one meeting to the next. So what was different?

Then it hit her. 'I'm not wearing a ring. He's the kind of man who checks. And now I'm fair game. Oh, no!'

She tried to shrug it off.

Mrs Lyristakis stirred a little more and opened her eyes. Caitlin watched her, her expression as reassuring as she could make it, but said nothing.

I'm not going to tell her about the kids yet, not when I know so little, not unless she asks…and I hope she doesn't.

But Mrs Lyristakis did. Not in coherent words, but the pull on Caitlin's hand and the evident struggle to find voice were very apparent. 'My…my—'

'They're both alive. They're in surgery,' was all she could truthfully say, pressing the warm, questing hand between her own palms. Physical care of the patient was more important. She got Mrs Lyristakis some ice chips to ease the dryness in her mouth and checked her urinary output, which was satisfactory.

At a quarter to eight, just as Caitlin was finally about to go off for her break, Mr Lyristakis arrived and so she spent fifteen minutes with him, did Mrs Lyristakis's observations again and then had another ten minutes on the phone up to Theatre at his request, trying to find out what was going on with the two boys, Alex and Nico, but all she got was a vague list of their injuries and a comment on 'still in surgery' about both of them.

'I can't tell you anything yet, Mr Lyristakis,' she reported to the distressed father. He was about fifty, with greying hair and a comfortably thickened waist, and his eyes were warm and dark and suffering. 'The paediatric surgeon who is overseeing the team will be down to see you as soon as he can.'

'Can I see them?'

'Not yet, I'm afraid. While you're waiting, why don't you try to rest a little, or grab something to eat?'

But he shook his head distractedly at this. 'I'm not hungry…'

'Then sit with your wife. You don't need to say anything. Just sit and hold her hand. The reassurance will do a lot for her.'

'But we're separated,' he suddenly blurted in his accented English. 'Since just before Christmas.'

'Oh, I see…'

'At least… It was all her idea. I didn't want it.'

Well, I could really get into trouble over this further down the line, but… 'She's not thinking about that at the moment, I'm sure,' Caitlin told him. 'You're the father of her boys. She needs you.'

He nodded vaguely, as if still too bewildered by everything to take anything in properly, and Caitlin watched him as she checked Mrs Lyristakis's surgical site, and couldn't help feeling a rush of hope when she saw him sit at his wife's side and take her hand. Mrs Lyristakis's eyes lingered on her husband for a moment and then she gave a faint smile. There was definitely an answering pressure, too. She wasn't pulling her hand away.

Caitlin felt her eyes mist over and her throat tighten, not sure why she found the sight such an emotional one.

At nine o'clock she was overdue for checking Mrs Reid and Mrs Best, then had to handle another admission, following emergency surgery, and she saw the possibility of getting any break at all disappearing rapidly into the distance. An hour later, with the shift nearly over, she accepted the inevitable. Things had just been flat out, and each of her patients needed checking again.

Mrs Best's grogginess following surgery had worn off now, and she was feeling anxious about William. 'I don't understand why Dr Ferguson hasn't come,' she complained impatiently to Caitlin, and the latter quite understood her concern. 'I've only had one report on William from a nurse…'

Me, actually, Caitlin thought, but she was obviously too woozy to notice my face. She didn't bother to clarify the point.

'And she just had it second-hand, although it seemed to be good news. I was told Dr Ferguson was in emergency surgery, but that was hours ago. He can't *still* be!'

'I'm afraid he is,' Caitlin corrected soberly.

'*Another* operation?'

'No, the same one. At least, there are two of them. Two patients. I mustn't say too much, but it was a car accident and we have the mother on this ward.'

'Oh, no! Just when the tide has turned for me, some other parents are having to go through hell…'

Speaking of hell… Angus looked like it a few minutes later

when he finally turned up while Caitlin was still with her patient. Mrs Best was down to four-hourly observations of her vital signs now, and she had been able to use a bedpan. Her wound site and dressing both looked good, too. Now both Caitlin and Mrs Best searched Angus's face for clues about the condition of the two boys, but that forbidding expression was set there as if it were carved in stone and it was impossible to read anything beyond weary preoccupation.

'I'm terribly sorry, Mrs Best,' he said immediately. 'I got held up, but I've just seen William and he's continuing to do beautifully. He's out of Recovery and into the isolation ward, as you know, and his new kidney has already proved it can function. He's having pain, of course, but we're easing that as much as we can. He asked about you and we told him you were fine.'

As he spoke, the forbidding weariness drained gradually from his face, and by the time he'd finished Caitlin knew that Mrs Best was no longer thinking of the two Lyristakis boys but only of her own son.

'And when can I see him?' she said. 'How long will he be in pain?'

'It should subside significantly by the end of tomorrow. As for seeing him, tomorrow morning we'll get an orderly and a wheelchair to take you down. The main thing to guard against, of course, is infection. So we'll need to have you gowned and capped and masked at this stage.'

Caitlin finished her work and slipped out, receiving only a vague nod from Angus—not that she'd expected or wanted anything more. She was impressed by his bedside manner, though. After what must have been a gruelling stint of surgery, on top of a late finish last night and an early start today, his focus on Mrs Best and her concern for her son had been total, and he'd answered several more questions from her clearly and cheerfully, with no attempt to rush the process.

After spending some minutes with Mrs Reid, as she was

finding little relief from her pain and discomfort at the moment, Caitlin returned to Mrs Lyristakis and encountered Angus once again. This time her heart flipped at the sight of him. He must be telling Vasilios Lyristakis about the condition of his sons.

I won't go in, she decided, doing an unobtrusive about-face in the doorway. They don't need a nurse fussing about while they're listening to what he has to say.

Fifteen minutes later, though, she waylaid Angus at the nurses' station as he was on his way out of the ward.

'Wait, please, Angus!'

He turned, and she saw at once that she'd disrupted a focused train of thought. 'Hmm?' he said.

'You look like you're held together by a few bits of string,' she told him bluntly, then realised that that was not at all the sort of thing you said to senior surgeons, even if they were related to you by marriage. Would there be an explosion? It might be good if there was. The air between them definitely needed clearing somehow. It was still thick with tangled feelings.

But no explosion came. 'Make that string and coffee and I'd agree with you,' he drawled. 'Could I have a cup? You make it *exactly* how I like it!'

'Of course…if you don't think you'd be better off heading straight for bed.'

'I can't go to bed for at least an hour and a half,' he answered solemnly.

'Oh, no! Do you have—?'

'It's New Year's Eve.'

'Hell, I'd almost forgotten!'

'So had I until a few minutes ago.'

'But tell me about the boys, Angus,' she begged. 'You were in there with the Lyristakises for a good twenty minutes. Will they live?'

'One will, but the other…' He trailed off, then exploded

suddenly, 'The other will, too, damn it! But that's my own stubbornness talking, it's not a clinical evaluation of his condition.'

'That bad?'

'Bad,' he agreed. 'If they both do recover, though, they should recover without any mental or physical handicap. Miraculously, there's no brain or spinal damage. Just a lot of broken bones and some hellish internal injuries. They'll both need follow-up surgery, too, because some of what we've done tonight is only temporary. It was bloody hard, telling Mr and Mrs Lyristakis about it.'

He had followed her into the tiny ward kitchen and was watching her absently as she got some rather stale perked coffee and pepped it up in the microwave with the scalded milk he liked. She was aware of his restlessness. His hand drummed on the counter-top then reached to rub at the nape of his neck, where his short hair emphasised the clean lines of his head. His strong shoulders rolled as he moved lower to massage away a point of tension in his spine.

He went on, as if he was testing his thoughts aloud, 'I hate the moment when I finish, when I've said it all, answered all their terrible, helpless questions, and they're just *left* with it.'

'*We* are, you mean,' she couldn't help pointing out. 'No matter how well you've handled it, you surgeons then disappear at that point and we're left trying to help them make sense of it, and deal with it, and stay sane through it.' She stopped, then added quickly, 'Sorry, Angus, I shouldn't have said that.'

'No, actually, I'm very interested in your perceptions.'

'Well, it wasn't meant as a criticism, nor as one upmanship. I think surgeons are amazing people. *I* couldn't do your job! I'm just saying—'

'That's OK,' he told her, fixing his dark eyes on hers. 'It's OK, Caitlin. You couldn't do my job and I couldn't do yours.' His voice had a husky little catch in it, and she felt the strength drain from her legs purely because of his nearness. 'And if you think I don't realise that we leave half the *really* hard emotional stuff to you lot,' he finished, 'then you're wrong!'

'Here's your coffee,' she said weakly, appalled at the way he confused her, probed to the heart of her, set her senses on fire…

CHAPTER SIX

ANGUS was waiting for Caitlin near the lifts when she came off duty. He'd loosened his plain white shirt around the neck, exposing his olive-skinned throat and the first hint of some dark hair. He was prowling, restless, fatigued, tense—until he saw her.

Then he stepped forward purposefully. 'Hello.'

'Hi.' She wasn't pleased to see him, and didn't try to disguise it. 'I hope you weren't waiting for me.'

He gave a crooked grin as he drawled, 'I know.'

'Then why are you?'

'Because it's New Year's Eve.'

'I'm aware of that!'

'So you've got something on, have you?'

'A party. But I doubt I'll go,' she admitted. Somehow she immediately found it easier to be honest than to pretend with Rachel's brother. Just as if they were friends, as he'd said last night. 'It's miles away,' she went on. 'And I don't have a car.'

'Really? Then how do you get around? To and from work?'

'I have a motorbike.'

He raised his eyebrows.

'I'm not exactly a heavy-duty motorcycle mama,' she drawled with a crooked smile. 'It's only a little Honda. And not much fun for long drives.'

'Do you feel safe on it in the city at night?'

'No, actually.'

'It must restrict your social life, then.'

'I don't go out at night much, except when Scott's down, and then we use his car. That is...' She realised what she'd said and pressed her fingers to her mouth, then let them fall. 'I *used* to…'

'You're missing him, aren't you?'

'No,' she said too quickly, then, 'Yes. That is, it takes getting used to. Not being engaged. Not being involved.'

'Of course it does. Come out with me, then,' he offered rather lazily.

'No!'

'Give me one good reason why not.'

'You're not supposed to say that!' He was bulldozing her, standing too close again as he leaned one elbow against the wall, waiting for the lift.

'*You're* supposed to get in first with a plausible excuse,' he countered. 'Like you're washing your hair or something. If you just say, *no* it sounds like you're frightened of something.'

'You *know* what I'm frightened of, Angus,' she said in a low voice.

'Yes, and I wish you weren't. Please, don't be, Caitlin. I'm not a monster. And I'm not a fool. I know this is too soon for you. I've had what was termed a "transitional relationship" and, believe me, it's not something I'm anxious to repeat! I promise I'm not trying to get you into bed.'

'Then what *are* you trying to do?'

'Hell, I'm not sure.' He swore under his breath. 'Get to know you a little better. You're my sister's sister-in-law. Will that do?'

'The answer's still no, Angus.'

He let out a controlled sigh, then shrugged. 'If that's what you want.'

It wasn't. Physically, she was intensely attracted to him, to every inch of his starkly masculine form, but it scared her, despite what he'd said. She had no doubt he'd respect the physical limits she set. What she distrusted was her own ability to set them. And she'd heard of transitional relationships!

One lift was way down on the ground floor, heading upwards. The other was also heading upwards unfortunately, and was almost here. Its doors opened to disgorge Greg Snow, and when he came straight up to her with all the subtlety of a bull eyeing an open gate she knew he'd been on the prowl for an off-duty nurse to help him see in the New Year…and probably see him through tomorrow's hangover as well.

'Waiting for me, I hope?' His unsubtle variation on her own line to Angus.

It was too much. Whatever the problems in her relationship with Scott, his ring and her clear status as a woman already spoken for had given her protection from men like this which she hadn't even understood or valued until it was gone.

'I'm sorry, Dr Snow, but I wasn't waiting for you,' she said, firm and polite. 'I was on my way—'

'Out with me,' Angus came in, smiling at Greg as he took her arm in his.

Greg shrugged, smiled feebly and turned towards Ward 6B, where two more nurses were just coming off duty.

A second lift arrived, and Angus pulled her into it before she heard Greg's opener this time around. She'd finished with Greg, but she hadn't finished with Angus. As soon as the lift doors had closed, she rounded on him.

'If you think I'm going to thank you for that…!'

'You don't enjoy being rescued?'

'Not when it's out of the frying pan and into the fire.'

Now he was as angry as she was. 'Don't pretend your response to me is anything like your response to Greg Snow,' he said sharply. 'Do us both a favour! I'm trying to be honest with you about all this, Caitlin. Tell me I'm wrong and I'll give up,' he said. 'Just answer me once and for all.'

He took a step towards her and she was at once surrounded by the aura of him—his scent, his masculinity, the indefinable but powerful pull he had on every one of her senses.

He wants me to admit I'd sleep with him.

And she knew she'd have to lie to deny it.

I can't! I'll admit it when he asks.

Steeled for the revelation, she was amazed to hear a far less challenging question.

'Does the simple thought of spending an hour or two in my company repel you?' he demanded quietly.

'No…' She was so relieved at getting away with the simple word that she hardly understood the message sent by her hot cheeks and her glittering eyes. 'No, it doesn't repel me at all.'

'Then come out with me. We'll get something to eat. We'll dance. We'll see in the New Year. And at the end of it I'll drive you home. No strings.'

Had it been a mistake to have said yes? Caitlin didn't think so at first. Now that she'd committed herself, she was actually able to relax in Angus's company.

Since she had brought clothes with her on the off chance that she had the energy for the party in Sylvania, she disappeared into the visitors' cloakroom on the ground floor to put them on. Silk pants in flowing peacock colours, because she'd anticipated having to ride the bike, with a simple matching top, sleeveless and cut in a gentle curve across her lightly tanned collar-bone. Low-heeled black satin shoes. Just a little make-up.

The top-floor nightclub of the Hotel Australasia, down near Circular Quay, was packed, and Caitlin wondered just how Angus could be so sure they'd get in. They did get in, though, at once, despite the press of extravagantly dressed hopefuls who were being held back by an alarmingly large and handsome bouncer.

When they were seated with large, bubbly drinks ten minutes later at one of the best tables in the entire establishment, right next to windows which overlooked half the harbour, she couldn't resist a comment. 'So, what did you have to do for this? Save the hotel owner's life?'

He laughed. It did wonderful things to his face. His eyes

were alive and soft, his jaw strong and clean, as he raised his head.

'No,' he answered, still grinning. 'I guess you've never heard the details of Rachel and Gordon's romance, then?'

'Not really. I know they met here in Sydney, after he was back from his year's field research in Antarctica.'

'Think of it, Caitlin, an Antarctic winter with no women in his research team. The team all came in here at opening time late one afternoon to celebrate their return to civilisation. The first thing Gordon heard was my sister bawling out one of the staff, who'd been knocking off nips of spirits on the sly. She was managing this place then, and she has quite a line in sarcasm when she has to.

'Since it's best known as a nightclub, not many people get here so early and she didn't realise there were any customers to overhear. Anyway, Gordon was deeply impressed by her performance—which I can only put down to his long deprivation of female company. He stayed till closing then asked her out, and came back every night until she finally agreed. The rest is history. You really haven't heard the story?'

'Gordon was probably too embarrassed! Who'd have thought a shy scientist like him...'

'Never underestimate the power of, well, shall I say true love, or the Antarctic winter?'

'The winter,' she suggested quickly.

He shrugged, and his glance called her a coward. She was when it came to his effect on her!

'So Rachel managed this place until they moved to Canberra last summer after they got married,' he finished. 'And I spent quite a bit of time here two years ago when I was in Sydney for a three-month stretch. It has good food, from its own kitchen. Are you hungry?'

'Actually, I'm *ravenous*!' She'd had precisely one cheese and lettuce sandwich and two shortbread biscuits since breakfast. 'I could eat...I don't know...anything!'

'Lobster? Caviar? Truffle pâté?'

'I think so.'

'But which?'

'I meant all three!'

'Coming up, then.'

She didn't really take him seriously, though, until—after he'd whispered something in a waiter's ear—an enormous platter of hot and cold savouries arrived, containing the three luxuries he had mentioned and much more besides.

'Angus, how did you—?'

'I know the menu pretty well, and for supper at midnight this is the best thing on it.'

'Midnight? I suppose it is!'

It was, in fact, exactly midnight. The music had fallen silent now, and everyone joined with the nightclub's DJ in counting down the final ten seconds of the outgoing year. Streamers were thrown. Paper party blowers filled the air with raucous, explosive sound. Fireworks burst over the Harbour. And everyone in the place found the person they had come here to kiss, or looked for someone who was standing by themselves with lonely lips.

Caitlin met Angus's eye and looked quickly away. No! Absolutely *not*! Not even a sisterly peck! She didn't dare to look up for some moments more, although her thoughts were replaying Sunday like a video. She filled her mouth shamelessly with a crumbling savoury to make the thing manifestly impossible and didn't relax until, against the background of everyone singing 'Auld Lang Syne', she heard him toast on a lazy drawl, with a raised glass, 'Happy New Year, Caitlin.'

'As to that,' she told him not quite steadily, raising her glass too, clinking it with his and taking a big gulp, 'all I ask is that it gets off to a passable start!'

'Then let's dance.' His deceptively lazy glance dared her to think of an excuse.

She couldn't. 'All right.'

He *could* dance, too. Not just the amorphous hopping about that anyone with a vestigial sense of body rhythm could manage, but real rock and roll dancing that you couldn't do unless you'd been taught—which *she* had, by an enthusiastic gym teacher at school, but where had *he* picked it up?

He didn't give her time to ask because as soon as he discovered that she could mesh her movements with his he put on the full show, twirling her out along his arm, tossing her in the air and making her breathless with effort and pleasure.

Both were disappointed when the two rock and roll numbers finished and the DJ announced, 'Now for a change of mood, people.'

A slow number.

No, thank you! thought Caitlin at once, and was intensely relieved when Angus drawled, 'I'll save you that, shall I?'

'If you don't mind.'

'Rock and roll's my forte, anyway. Rachel made me partner her for a couple of years at dance lessons when we were kids.'

'I wondered how you'd learned. And I'm amazed you're still friends!'

'Believe me, there were times when we weren't! Dance lessons are not something fifteen-year-old boys boast about at school, as you're no doubt aware. But Rachel can be persuasive.'

'So I understand from her husband!'

'Let's get some fresh air.'

'Oh, is there a terrace?'

It must be frighteningly high if there was because they were on the twentieth floor.

'Better than a terrace,' he promised.

They sidled their way off the increasingly crowded dance floor and through the tables at the side and she couldn't work out what was happening—this *wasn't* the way to the exit—until he reached the swing doors to the kitchen and pushed them open.

Caitlin had never been in a restaurant kitchen before. Angus obviously had, though. The place was alive with noise and movement—the clang of an oven door, the sizzle of steak on a grill, the shouting of new orders by three waiters at once. Caitlin would have stood there near the busy door, getting in everyone's way, but Angus edged her around towards the service lift and then caught the head chef's eye. 'Chris!'

'Hello, Angus.' Contrary to all known stereotypes of the culinary profession, he was wiry, quite thin, and red-haired. 'How's it going? You're living in Sydney now, right?'

'Since October.'

'Less than a year after Rachel deserts us for Canberra.'

'I know. Crazy, isn't it? But that's life. She and I haven't actually lived in the same city for over fifteen years.'

'Have you come for a free feed?'

Angus laughed. It was such a rich sound, and softened his face so much. 'No,' he said. 'I paid.'

'You should have let me know you were here.'

'I'm doing that now.'

'I meant before.'

'I knew you'd be busy. Now, though, Caitlin and I wanted some fresh air.'

'Caitlin. Hi.' Chris nodded.

She managed a passable greeting but felt awkward, knowing the red-haired chef would assume she was someone important, and she had to suppress an absurd urge to clarify the issue at once.

We're not seriously involved. Until yesterday—didn't seem possible it was only yesterday—I was engaged to someone else.

But that would have been horribly gauche, and Chris was far too busy to be remotely interested in such niceties. He reached into his pocket, pulled out some keys and tossed them at once to Angus, startling Caitlin into a gasp and a giggle.

'Have you had dessert?' Chris asked them.

'No, we haven't.'

'Then take these…' he picked up two glass dishes of apricot and almond mousse, '…and eat them outside.'

Still laughing, Caitlin took the proffered desserts and realised that, indeed, she was still hungry.

'Are you sure, Chris?' Angus asked.

'Go on. We'll be throwing them out. Not enough orders. They're all going for the chocolate and hazelnut torte, and the tiramisu.'

'Thanks.'

'Don't forget to give me back the keys, and I might have a minute then to hear more about how Rachel's getting on. Didn't I hear she was pregnant?'

'Yes, due in a couple of months.'

'Great!'

He turned from them and headed for the big wall oven, while Angus started towards the large service lift. Caitlin still didn't know where they were going.

'Careful, the floor can be slippery,' he told her as he pressed the lift button. Somewhere below she heard the lift machinery grinding into action.

Three minutes later, after turning a key in an unobtrusive lock on the lift control panel, Angus ushered her onto the roof. It wasn't a public garden, but the business end of the luxury hotel where vents and air-conditioning units and lift housings vied for space. Bordering the expanse of rather grungy cement, there was a waist-high parapet so it was perfectly safe… and about as romantic as a trysting place for alley cats, which was *just fine* with Caitlin tonight! The last thing she wanted was moonlight, music and greenery.

Yet, she soon decided, it was fabulous. Quirky. Private. Special. It showed a side of Angus that she'd almost forgotten about these past few days. The side of him that could make her laugh as they searched her parents' beach-side garden for a child's forgotten toy. The side of him that was happy to get up at six on a summer morning to watch the sun over the sea.

Here, now, a week or so later—surely it had to be longer—they could see the harbour spread out almost below them, with its jostling party boats, a cruise ship or two and the Opera House and Luna Park all lit up. The bridge seemed to tower just over their heads and the buildings of the city reached up behind them into a blue, misty darkness that had the beauty of a carefully lit stage set.

They could hear sounds of revelry coming from all over the place, as well as the noise of cars and crowds leaving Circular Quay and the Opera House steps after the fireworks. None of the noise was too close, though, and there was a delicious sense of secrecy about this space.

'Shall we sit?' he invited, gesturing at a long metal housing. Caitlin couldn't even guess what it might contain. The emergency generator?

'Doesn't look very clean,' she pointed out.

But he was already spreading out two shiny green plastic garbage bags he must have snaffled from the pile near the lift downstairs. She sat on one and then realised aloud, 'We don't have spoons for the mousse.'

As if on cue, a waiter appeared out of the lift, bringing not only spoons but two glasses of champagne as well. 'The boss decided he didn't have you properly equipped.'

When he had gone again Caitlin threw back her head and laughed, delighted at the setting. 'This is amazing, Angus! When you said fresh air…' She reached across to take a spoon of the creamy mousse and savoured it appreciatively on her tongue.

'Rachel and I used to do this. She put in a very long day because the place is normally open from five in the afternoon until four in the morning. She could usually only get away for ten minutes at a stretch, and by eleven or so she was longing for fresh air.'

'I don't blame her. It's fabulous! It *is* fresh, too, because there's a sea breeze blowing over the water.'

'In New York people come up to these sorts of places in summer. The roofs of the apartment buildings are surfaced with bitumen-coated paper. New Yorkers lay out their towels and sunbake on their "tar beach".'

'Poor things!' she said fervently, thinking of Coogee and Maroubra and Bondi and all the other glorious beaches in Sydney, as well as all up and down the New South Wales coast from Byron Bay to Eden.

He laughed. 'I thought you said you liked this!'

'Well, after midnight, alone and with this glorious backdrop of city lights, yes. It's delightful. And so is this mousse. But not in the heat of the day with half a dozen other people as a beach substitute.'

He picked up his champagne. 'Do we need to toast again?'

'Yes,' she told him promptly. 'To your persistence, perhaps. I—I'm glad you forced the issue, Angus, and made me come. I'm having a great time.'

Their eyes met, and all of a sudden, once again, it was dangerous. There was an immediate, mutual and unworded agreement not to linger. As soon as champagne and mousse were gone he stood up, folded his plastic bag and looked towards the lift. Caitlin folded her bag, too, and they waited together, very definitely not close enough to touch, while the hollow, metallic sound from the lift well signalled its approach.

'I think you'd better take me home, Angus,' she told him, too brightly.

'I think so, too,' he agreed, his voice dark and low.

CHAPTER SEVEN

'How was your Christmas?' Chief of Surgery David Lyle-Smith said to Angus early on New Year's Day as he sat back in his leather office chair.

'It seems like weeks ago,' Angus answered truthfully, seated opposite him, across a large desk. He was well practised at fighting off fatigue, but at times it wasn't easy. 'Ask me about New Year instead!'

'New Year?' Dr Lyle-Smith echoed with a wry look. 'Have we had that already? I've been too busy to notice! I certainly haven't made any resolutions.'

'I've made one,' Angus admitted, smiling to himself as he thought about last night.

'Oh, really?'

'Yes. To take things slowly.'

'Hmm.'

David didn't seem particularly interested. Why should he be? It was a cryptic and not particularly earth-shattering announcement. Angus was thinking of Caitlin, of course. Last night had been just right. They hadn't kissed. They'd barely touched. They'd just ended the evening knowing each other a little better than before.

And he knew that was what she needed. No rush. No hurry. Now that she'd ended her engagement to Scott, Angus's turmoil on the issue had subsided and he felt relaxed and confident. A few days ago the whole thing had seemed like an impossible mess, with his own feelings the most misguided element of all. But now, despite the fact that he wanted her, wanted her bright summery loveliness and her steadfast inner glow as he hadn't wanted a woman since…no, as he hadn't wanted a woman *ever*…the urgency and turmoil had gone.

'I'm glad I ran into you, Angus,' David was saying. 'I'd have phoned you at home if I hadn't.'

They had met up in the main foyer when Angus was on his way in to see patients, and now he'd been sidetracked by his chief to the latter's office for 'a quick word'. Something trivial, Angus had at first assumed, but now, suddenly, alarm bells were ringing. David wasn't given to private conferences in his office at short notice without good reason.

'You know Michael Bowen over at West Sydney, don't you?' David asked.

'We've met,' Angus agreed cautiously. Dr Bowen was also a paediatric surgeon and, like Angus, interested in transplant surgery.

'He's very good. Nice man, too. The thing is, he's had a bit of bad luck and I think, with your co-operation, Angus, it's going to turn into a very good opportunity for Southshore…'

'Really? Give me the details! You've got me interested now.'

Half an hour later, when he emerged from David's office, Angus had a whole slew of new things to do, an 'excellent and unexpected opportunity' to adjust to, one that David Lyle-Smith had made it abundantly clear Angus could not risk refusing, and the dawning understanding that his first and only New Year's resolution thus far was shortly about to be shot down in flames.

At the moment he wasn't remotely happy about the prospect of any of it.

In the ward on the afternoon of New Year's Day, Caitlin was very conscious of the fact that Angus had reason to turn up here without warning, and at first she was as jumpy as a cat. Memories of last night kept ambushing her. Nice memories.

Memories that *should* have been safe because she and Angus hadn't even kissed, only she was starting to understand in a way she never had with Scott that there was much more to intimacy than physical contact.

Fortunately, however, there was too much nursing to do for this state of distraction to last for long. Patient numbers were still low but so were staff numbers and Caitlin was kept busy with her trio of women.

Mrs Reid was still receiving no food orally but was too ill to wish for anything more substantial, and all the staff would have liked to see her showing more energy at this stage. Everyone was hoping for a quick recovery from the surgery itself and an improvement in her pain control to allow her some time at home as soon as possible. She was particularly quiet and thoughtful today, though, was refusing an increased dose of narcotics because she wanted to be alert enough to think and Stevie Reid hadn't been in yet, according to the outgoing staff.

One of Betty's first requests to Caitlin was for pen and paper, and for the next hour she sat up in bed as high as she was allowed and thought and effortfully scribbled things down in her clumsy, erratic handwriting.

Caitlin thought, She's making plans while she still can. Her will, perhaps? Or what she wants for her funeral? She's just doing what needs to be done, quietly embracing it, I guess.

For some reason, some lines from the biblical book of Ecclesiastes came into her mind. 'For everything there is a season…' An American folk group had made them into a song back in the 1960s, and the melody started going round and round in Caitlin's head.

She was unconsciously humming it aloud as she came back from emptying Mrs Reid's catheter bag at half past four, ''And a time for every purpose under heaven.''

But now there was a sudden movement in the doorway of Mrs Reid's room, and Stevie came hurrying out. 'Sorry, Mum,

I just need the toilet,' she was saying in a strangled voice, and her emotion broke almost before she had cleared the doorway.

Entering the room, Caitlin found that Mrs Reid was under no illusion about the reason for the sudden departure. She was gazing helplessly after her daughter, and wearing a complex expression, creased with worry now, as well as pain. 'Oh…dear… That wasn't…what I wanted to happen…'

'Have you been scolding her?' Caitlin said gently, with a sympathetic twinkle in her eye.

'Talking to her…about my funeral. I asked her something… Well, it's up to her. I must…tell her that…as soon as she comes back.'

Caitlin re-attached the bag and checked that it would fill properly. She wondered whether to ask Betty for more detail, but the sixty-two year old woman seemed immersed in thought once again and in no need of thrashing through her problems aloud.

Stevie, though… She was prowling back and forth in the corridor, blowing her nose and pretending to study various health or nature posters on the walls if anyone came past as she fought back her tears. When she saw Caitlin, however, she turned. 'Mum saw that I was upset, didn't she?'

'Yes, she did.'

'I didn't want her to. She'll think I don't want to do it. You see, she's asked me to sing at her funeral.'

Her thin control broke again and several tissues were seized on with desperate need.

'And you *do* want to?'

'Oh…' Stevie spread her hands. '"Want" isn't the word. I'm so happy that she thought of it, and so afraid that I'll just open my mouth and nothing will come but crying. Yet if I could do it, and make it good…It'd be *right*, because she loves my singing.'

'Do you sing professionally?' Caitlin asked, seeing that talking was calming Stevie down.

The latter smiled. 'Well, we pay ourselves any profit from our shows, but I wouldn't call it a profession. We all do other things as well. It's a women's country music band called Lizzy in the Kitchen…which gives you an idea where most of us practise!'

'Your mum said to me just now that she won't ask you to do it if you don't want to,' Caitlin said, more seriously now. 'I think you should talk about it with her as openly as you can, not try to hide your doubts and fears. The thing is, you know, no one will mind at the funeral if you *do* cry.'

'Yes, yes, you're right, of course. It was silly to run out like that, but she caught me by surprise. She's facing this so well it sometimes seems wrong to me. That song you were singing just now…'

'Oh, I'm sorry, was I singing aloud?'

Stevie nodded. 'Yes, and don't be sorry about it. It struck a chord for me. Mum seems to have accepted that this is her "season" but I haven't yet.'

'You're the one who has to go on living,' Caitlin answered.

It was what the Reids' GP, Julius Marr, had said the other day. A trite comment, perhaps, worn from overuse, but true all the same. It was how she felt about her own life at the moment. She and Scott weren't together any more, and she just had to go on living until she fully worked out what that meant.

Meanwhile, Mrs Lyristakis was far more alert tonight than she had been yesterday, and her physical suffering took a clear second place to the anxiety she felt over her boys. The one positive thing was the presence of her husband. Vasilios Lyristakis hadn't left the hospital since his arrival last night. He had slept for several hours in the chair beside Mrs Lyristakis's bed and spent the rest of the night in the paediatric intensive care unit with his sons, and he looked exhausted now.

'Why don't you go and get some proper sleep?' Caitlin

suggested gently to him as she checked Mrs Lyristakis's dressing at just after nine.

'Is it…necessary?' he wanted to know. His English was almost perfect but quite strongly accented. He glanced at his wife.

Caitlin answered, 'No, it's not necessary. You're welcome to stay…if you'd like him to, Mrs Lyristakis.'

It was a delicate issue. Her sympathy had been aroused by his obvious unhappiness over his wife's desire to separate, but her first duty was to her patient and if Mrs Lyristakis wanted him to leave then he would have to do so.

Caitlin had reported to the night staff yesterday that the couple were separated, but they'd seen no sign that Mrs Lyristakis was rejecting her husband's presence and it certainly didn't look as if she considered their marriage over at the moment. She had seized her husband's hand and was speaking fervent words to him in Greek. A moment later he bent to her face and they kissed with clumsy passion as tears ran down both their cheeks.

'I'm staying,' he announced.

Mrs Lyristakis added incoherently, 'I've been crazy. That's finished now. I'm not letting this beautiful man out of my sight.'

Vasilios Lyristakis wasn't particularly beautiful in anyone's book, but when he smiled he almost glowed and Caitlin thought, What a wonderful happy ending! Then Angus walked into the ward fifteen minutes later with a grim reminder that this wasn't the end at all.

'Are both the Lyristakises here?' he asked Caitlin at the nurses' station, dispensing with such superfluities as 'hello'. He didn't seem to consider it necessary.

'Yes, and cooing together like a pair of doves,' she answered. 'Why? You didn't think we'd have discharged her, did you?'

'No, but I half expected to hear she'd been transferred to

the ICU or something similar, the way my day has been.' His tight expression told her that this wasn't the first half of a joke, and she made a sound of dismay before he even finished his explanation, already on his way to Fotini Lyristakis's room. 'You see, I've just finished another stint of surgery on Alex.'

Nothing simple either, from the look of him. His eyes were on fire and he hadn't shaved today. His jaw was darkly shadowed, emphasising its square strength.

For absolutely no good reason at all, Caitlin looked at the wall clock and realised, It's a quarter past nine. Just over a week…a whole, long action-filled week or a tiny, insignificant interval of eight days, depending on how you chose to look at it…since Angus and I first met. Too much had happened since then. Perhaps it wasn't surprising that her insides churned inside every time she saw him.

On entering Mrs Lyristakis's room, Angus closed the door behind him and didn't emerge for half an hour, which had Laurel, Brooke and Caitlin all feeling anxious and miserable on their patient's behalf.

'Internal bleeding,' Brooke theorised uselessly. 'It must be that. So, if it's repaired now, he could be out of danger in a couple of days and—'

'Don't, Brooke,' Laurel said firmly. 'We have to do *our* jobs, and not the jobs of the nurses in PICU. I just hope Hunterdon gives her the go-ahead to visit them tomorrow…and thank goodness the husband seems so caring!'

A visit to her son had certainly done wonders for Elise Best. Her side of the transplant surgery had been a simple procedure and she would be discharged by Monday or Tuesday. Meanwhile, she had been able to take a wheelchair down to the small transplant ward on the fifth floor this morning for the first time to see William, and as that was something which would help his own recovery it would now be allowed whenever possible.

In fact, she'd just got back from kissing him goodnight.

'The precautions against infection are scary,' she told Caitlin, while having her temperature and pulse checked. 'I assumed at first that he'd be in Intensive Care, but when they told me that was too *risky*... I know it's not really that way, but it seemed as if Dr Ferguson was saying he was *too sick* to be in the ICU.'

'I know.' Caitlin nodded. 'But you do understand the problem with infection, don't you?'

'Oh, yes! Dr Ferguson explained all that very clearly. The drugs William's on to stop his body rejecting the kidney weaken his immune system.'

'But once he's recovered from the surgery, they'll find the best drug regime to keep a balance between rejection and vulnerability to infection.'

'And that seems so much easier and more positive than bringing him in for that terrible, inexorable dialysis three times a week. Somehow he just never handled it well, and when Dr Ferguson told me that he and Dr Godwin didn't want to wait until the new year for the transplant after all... Oh, thank God it's over!'

Caitlin couldn't help feeling that way, too, as she came off duty at eleven and went down in the lift. I need some sleep! she thought.

On the ground floor Angus had his finger on the 'up' button, but turned away from the lift as soon as he saw her.

'I almost missed you,' he said.

'You weren't looking for me?'

'Yes, I was.'

The calm admission made her crack. 'Why? Why, Angus? Can't you see I'm not ready for this?'

She didn't realise how her voice had risen until she heard it echo in the wide space of the main foyer and saw the security man on duty look up from his desk. Angus saw the man's sudden interest, too. City hospitals were security-conscious. They had to be. The last thing either Angus or Caitlin wanted was a big, public blow-up, as if they were a couple of drunken, brawling casualty admissions.

'Come for a coffee?' Angus said quietly.

'No!'

'There's something I have to tell you.'

'Can't it wait? I'm very tired.' She sounded short-tempered, and knew it. Another minute of her mood and he wouldn't *want* to be with her!

But he said very seriously, 'No, it can't wait. That's the whole problem.'

Two minutes later, she was sitting in the passenger seat of his familiar car. She didn't realise they were going to his place until he dived into the underground car park beneath an elegant new block of units.

'Angus…' she protested at once.

'Listen!' He rounded on her. The tyres squealed as he turned the wheel to enter his numbered space. 'Do you really think I'm going to force something on you that you don't want? My sister's married to your brother, for heaven's sake!' He switched off the engine and opened the door. Caitlin did the same. 'I could hardly get away with cold-blooded seduction, even if I was inclined to such things—which I'm not. If you think this situation is any easier for me than it is for you then you're wrong!'

'What situation, Angus?' she retorted wearily.

They were both out of the car now. The doors were closed. He'd slammed his, then he'd set his car alarm. She began to follow him to the lift. Lifts had been playing a significant role in their relationship lately, and it looked as if things were going to continue that way.

'You *know*!' he insisted. 'But I'll spell it out if that will help. I'm talking about the fact that we find each other extremely attractive, and yet you've just come out of a long-standing relationship so the timing is almost impossible. *That* situation, Caitlin. Have I got it wrong?'

'No, you haven't got it wrong,' she admitted.

'Good. We at least have a shared foundation from which to proceed,' he rasped, then didn't say another word until they'd reached his spacious flat.

It was the home of a successful single man who'd travelled widely—comfortable, clean, uncluttered and given his own stamp by the collection of pictures and knick-knacks he'd carefully picked out over the years. The long, squishy couch, upholstered in mahogany-hued leather, looked impossibly inviting, but she stayed standing, as if to sit might be considered a sexual overture.

'Coffee?' Angus offered at once.

'I won't sleep,' she answered truthfully. 'Just—'

'Hot chocolate, then?'

She had been going to ask for water, but hot chocolate, even in summer, sounded very nice. She nodded. 'Lovely…'

'Coming up.'

Restlessly, she followed him to the kitchen and watched him make it, as well as brewing up some coffee for himself. He poured his into a cup and added a generous dollop of milk then put both drinks in the microwave to make sure they were piping hot.

'Caitlin, I've been asked—well, *told*, actually, just this morning—to go to Los Angeles on a fellowship for four months.' He hadn't waited until they were settled with the drinks, and the words echoed very abruptly as they both stood in the kitchen.

'A fellowship! That's great, Angus,' she offered. 'When?'

'I'll have to leave a week from tomorrow. I don't expect the news to send you into a deep depression…' He gave an upside-down smile.

'No,' she agreed dutifully, although she felt unsettled, disappointed and already fearful about what might be coming next. It was sudden, to say the least.

His microwave pinged. The two stoneware mugs, which had been dancing sedately around the lit-up interior, came to a stop and he opened the door, gave hers a stir and handed it to her. Their fingers touched briefly. The silence was beginning to stretch out now.

'What do you want me to say, Angus?' she demanded desperately. 'The timing is terrible, but—'

'*That's* what I wanted you to say! The timing *is* terrible. I don't want to be merely the man who helps you get over Scott. The only way a relationship between us can possibly work, for *both* of us, is if we take things slowly, and now the chance to do that has been taken away from us.'

'Make it work?' she moaned. 'Angus, I can't think in those terms.'

'Damn, I *know* that!' He swore again, more darkly. 'You can't think in those terms, and I can't think in any other terms. Perhaps I'm too stubborn. I'm not prepared to fall victim to something as ultimately trivial as *timing*. Are you?'

'If you mean do I think so much else between a man and a woman is more important, like compatibility, and chemistry, and faithfulness, then, no. But, Angus, I can't! No matter what pressure you going away puts me under, it feels disloyal to Scott, to what we had, to move on from it so quickly. What we had ultimately wasn't right, but for a long time it was good and I don't want to dismiss that.'

Angus watched her staring down into her milky pool of chocolate and his stomach twisted. She looked so young, and she was. Twelve years his junior. And yet there was a maturity to her outlook that he'd recognised almost at once.

He saw it again now in the sober line of her full upper lip and the dark sweep of her lashes against the creamy pink background of her passion-warmed cheeks. She was speaking from the heart, tearing herself up over what she believed she owed to Scott. He was so painfully tempted to take a short cut, take the easy way out and *tell* her.

You're wasting your time. He doesn't deserve it. He was unfaithful to you even when you were wearing his ring. Bruising you, hurting you, while you didn't even know. You owe him *nothing* now! So forget him, and come to me.

And when the words stayed unspoken, he honestly didn't know... Was he acting nobly because he didn't want to see her hurt, to see her trust destroyed? Yes, there *was* that. Absolutely. He was astonished at how much he cared about her after so short a time.

But didn't his silence have more to do with the bottom line, and what *he* wanted? he demanded of himself, mistrusting his own motives, truly not knowing.

If he told her, she'd have to come to terms with it, which would take time—take time away from *him*—and in the circumstances he simply couldn't afford that. He was *not* going to be her transitional man!

In the end all he could say, and very stiffly, was, 'I'm not asking you to dismiss it. Just spend some time with me before I go. Are you off tomorrow?'

'Yes, but—'

'Then could we have the day together? Just the day? The sort of day I might spend with Rachel if she were here?'

'I'd like that, Angus,' she admitted very carefully, and it was actually more than he'd let himself hope for.

The phone rang. He knew who it would be. His old friend Adam in London, who existed on five hours' sleep a night and could never be convinced that anybody actually went to bed before midnight. It was only just on that now, and in London, of course, it was early afternoon. Talk about bad timing—again...

'Hello, Adam,' he said resignedly into the phone, then spent the next ten minutes trying to tactfully get the poor guy to hang up.

When he at last put down the phone and looked across at Caitlin on his leather couch she was fast asleep, her face smooth and untroubled, one cheek tickled by a rippling, wayward strand of spun gold hair and her warm pink mouth almost smiling. He must have watched her like that for several minutes before he very deliberately shook himself, stretched the tired muscles of his face and went in search of a pillow and blanket.

'Look at it this way,' Angus said, when the sun was bright the next morning. 'It saves us having to think of a time and place to meet today.'

'I've never done anything like this before!' Caitlin protested, still bleary eyed, clutching a fresh-scented pillow and hiding beneath a cotton blanket.

He must have put the pillow beneath her head and draped the blanket over her last night. Tugging at it, she found it was tucked beneath the couch cushions. So he'd actually bent over her and *tucked her in*!

Her hair was a bush, her uniform—yes, she'd actually slept the night in her uniform—had so many creases it would make a convincing road map of some densely populated European nation, and the only saving grace was that she'd been wearing no make-up yesterday so at least she didn't have eye rings like an insomniac panda.

Angus was grinning. 'I won't ask you how you slept.'

'Like a log, or I'd have phoned for a taxi the moment I stirred.'

'I know. That's why I didn't ask. Proves you have a clear conscience, doesn't it?'

'Angus…! Do *you*?' she teased. 'What did you put in that hot chocolate?'

'Nothing, I promise. Do you really think I'd drug you?' Like hers, his tone was light.

'I'm *hoping* you would, actually, if you were asked with a nice "please". I need caffeine!'

'Coming up. Want to take a shower while it's brewing?'

'Love to. What I *don't* want is to have to—'

'Get dressed in that attractively crushed and stale uniform,' he agreed, grinning. 'I've thought of that. You'll find an over-sized T-shirt and a scarf of my mother's draped over the bath-room towel rail, along with a clean towel. I expect you can put together something passably decent with those till I can get you home to change.'

She uttered a heartfelt, 'Thanks!' Then she barely waited till he'd safely disappeared into the kitchen.

His bathroom was heavenly. Clean and airy with a shower nozzle that seemed to dispense massage rather than water. She stayed beneath it for a sinful length of time and even sham-pooed her hair, then dried herself on a huge fluffy towel, blow-dried her hair and put on the big white T-shirt. It came nearly to her knees, so could be quite safely cinched in at her hips with the pink and purple silk scarf.

When she emerged at last, she found that Angus's flat had a shaded balcony, and he'd laid breakfast for them out there—orange juice, coffee, and croissants still warm from a nearby French patisserie. He also had the weekend edition of the *Sydney Morning Herald*.

'I despise conversation over breakfast,' he said cheerfully, unfolding the thick wad of newsprint. 'Which section would you like first?'

'Oh… *Spectrum*?' she suggested weakly, getting a glimpse of heaven.

They maintained a relaxed and completely pleasurable silence for the next hour.

The day promised to be another scorcher. The sun had be-gun to creep around the side of the building now to make a slowly expanding wedge of heat and light on the balcony. Very soon it would be uncomfortably hot.

'How about the beach?' Angus suggested.

'Perfect!'

Wearing baggy navy shorts and a white T-shirt, he drove her home to change and she invited him in, not wanting him to have to wait in a hot car. And she couldn't help contrasting his presence in her tiny flat with Scott's. Angus dominated it, dwarfed it, yet didn't look out of place as Scott always had— perhaps because Angus didn't seem to *feel* out of place.

When she emerged from her bathroom—as it was a studio flat there was no other private space to dress—she found him sitting on her low two-seater couch flipping through a book of Antarctic photography.

'From Gordon,' she told him. 'He wanted us to know how pitiless and beautiful it was.'

'Is it a place you'd like to go?'

'Oh, definitely! They have cruises there these days for your more intrepid species of tourist. But, then…' she smiled wryly, '…I'd like to go everywhere!'

'You could,' he pointed out. 'As a nurse, your skills and qualifications travel well, and Australian nurses have a very good reputation overseas.'

But she shook her head. 'I don't want to travel alone. I'm not looking for that sort of adventure. I'd like to share the experiences of travel with someone.'

'Just anyone?'

'No, the right friend, or— Well,' she interrupted herself quickly, 'someone important, anyway. And I'm patient. If it takes my whole life to get to the places on my list, so be it. It doesn't all have to happen *now*.'

'As far as *now* goes, then, are you ready?' He looked her up and down lazily.

She'd exchanged one white garment for another—a simple cotton jersey dress that was easy to fling on and off over a swimsuit. The black and mauve one-piece showed darker beneath the fine white fabric, and on her feet she wore open-toed purple plastic sandals.

'Think so. Oops, no, a beach towel, hat and sun-screen. I'm not ready at all!' She also packed a carry bag with something less casual to change into later on.

Five minutes later they were on their way to Bondi, where the hottest hours of the day slipped rapidly away on sand and in surf. They ate a late lunch of grilled seafood at an open-air café, where wet hair, purple plastic sandals and bare male legs were not considered too informal, then had another swim.

Through it all Angus said and did nothing lover-like, nothing that could have told her he wanted her. And yet she knew he did. What was it, then? Something in his eyes? Something in the way his body moved? Or was she only picking up the subtle chemistry that surrounded him because she felt that way herself?

Sitting on her towel and watching him emerge from the water to come towards her, Caitlin's heart lurched. Water streamed from his dark head. His shoulders were broad and tanned and his stomach was flat and hard. But her response to him was far more than mere awareness of his virile form.

Reaching her, he grinned with sheer pleasure and picked up his towel, his face disappearing beneath it as he towelled his hair into a damp, salty shock. And as he emerged she came very close to reaching up her arms for him, pulling him down to her, inviting him with her bare, warm limbs to hold her and kiss her and caress her.

She came *so* close! She *wanted* it! Wanted to know what his lips would feel like as they trailed down her neck and nuzzled the hot valley between her breasts. Wanted to discover the hair-roughened texture of his skin and the shape of his muscles beneath her fingers.

What's happening? she thought, her pulses clamouring. Is this being on the rebound? Wanting to anaesthetise my confusion by finding feelings for someone else? Am I just scared of being alone? Is Angus right? Is there a future in this if we can get over the bad timing of it? Or is it all a shallow illusion because I've been set adrift from what I thought was my future? That happens. It happens all the time…

He could tell something was wrong, but didn't say anything about it at first. They sat side by side on their towels, watching the crowds in the water, saying nothing. It was the first silence between them today that *hadn't* felt right, the first that had felt awkward and wrong and stiff.

In the end he was the first one to speak. 'I was going to suggest a gallery wander or a ferry ride, and then dinner,' he began slowly, 'but you look…tired and—'

'No, not tired,' she came in. The one thing she knew was real in their relationship, the one thing she fully trusted, was their honesty. 'Just ready to call it a day. It's been great, Angus.'

'It has, hasn't it?' He nodded. 'But you don't have to explain.'

They walked down a long side street back to his car, and the shimmering heat of tarred road and concrete footpath had chased away the water's coolness well before they reached it. When he opened the passenger door for her, the heat blasted out at her like an open furnace, and they ended up opening all four doors to let the faint sea breeze blow through and make the temperature bearable. His air-conditioning completed the job as they drove.

And perhaps it was the effect on her skin of a long buffeting by the surf, a bake by the sun and now the cool waft of the air-conditioning…or perhaps it wasn't anything to do with all that. All Caitlin knew was that her body ached for Angus with shocking intensity, and when he stopped outside her cream brick building and turned to her, already weaving some polite words about their day on his lips, the truth just spilled from her in a husky, suffering whisper.

'Angus, I want to kiss you so badly…'

His eyes probed her face. 'I wasn't going to,' he said.

'I—I know. And you shouldn't. You were right. We won't.'

'Damn it, Caitlin, don't keep talking about it. I'm only human…' He leaned across. 'Very, very human, sometimes…'

'I…think I must be, too,' she whispered hazily.

Their lips met. Their hands joined, and his thumbs ran across her fingers, caressing them. Then they let go again to make a hungry exploration of each other's bodies. His T-shirt was slightly damp, and beneath it she could feel the hard ridge of his spine and the rippling play of muscles on his back. Running her fingers higher, she found the hot curve of his neck and the soft prickles of short dark hair above his nape.

Meanwhile, he was slowly pulling the cotton jersey of her dress upwards, making her thigh thrill like silk beneath the teasing caress of his palm.

'Oh, Caitlin…' he murmured against her mouth, then parted her lips and drank the taste of her as if she alone might quench his savage summer thirst.

His hand had reached her waist now, and it was climbing higher, nudging the sensitive undersides of her breasts so that her nipples peaked almost painfully in her still faintly damp swimsuit. He discovered the fact for himself seconds later, and she heard the growl of satisfaction that emerged from deep in his throat.

Heard it…and then felt it swept from her mind as what he was doing to her swamped her senses completely.

Beneath the protective screen of her dress, he'd eased the fine straps of her swim-suit down her shoulders, and now he could claim her breasts completely, skin to skin, caressing the tender flesh, taking the rounded weights in his hand and running his forefinger along the incredibly sensitive curves where the underwire of her suit had rested.

She shuddered and felt her body's need clamour even louder. This car wasn't comfortable or private for what they were doing. It was hotting up again now that the engine was off. Her flat was a mere two flights of stairs away. They could so easily go upstairs and—

'Stop… Stop, Angus,' she managed, finding the tiny kernel of control that still remained.

Fighting herself more than him, she stiffened and froze her limbs, holding herself still with eyes closed. She felt his caressing grip slacken and slide away, and even the retreat of his hands was a delectable caress. After a moment he was back in the driver's seat, immobile, and she dared to open her eyes…to find him watching her.

'I'm sorry,' she blurted. 'I—I'm not playing—That *wasn't* a game!'

'I know,' he answered gravely.

'Good. Because I—'

'Go, Caitlin. Don't say any more. You don't need to. Thanks for today.'

'Thank *you*.' She fought her impulse to burble on with apologies and explanations. Incredibly, he seemed to understand.

'I'll see you tomorrow.'

'Tomorr—?'

'I'm taking you out to dinner. Do you think you'll be ready for it by then?'

'I—hope so.'

'Seven, then?'

'Seven.'

'I'll pick you up.' He gave a dry smile. 'Provided I'm ready for it by then myself.'

CHAPTER EIGHT

'SARAH, if you were so keen to spend time on Ward 6A, you could have just requested a transfer,' Caitlin teased her friend gently.

It was five o'clock on Monday afternoon, the hot summer sun and the hospital's large air-conditioning system were engaged in a titanic battle and an old friend from training days, Sarah McNulty, lay in the bed next to Fotini Lyristakis's, her short, red-rinsed hair tufting on the pillow. She was still drowsy from the pain medication which followed her emergency surgery.

It had been a shock to find her there when Caitlin had come on at three. Apparently Sarah had accidentally stepped out into the path of a passing four-wheel-drive in the early hours of that morning and had sustained a ruptured spleen and some liver damage in the process.

The full story wasn't known in detail, but Caitlin understood that Sarah and her boyfriend had been to a party and ended the evening in an argument on the footpath in front of their friend's house. In the heat of the moment, and after several drinks, Sarah had started off across the street without looking and—

Caitlin shuddered, and refused to look at the picture her mind created out of the facts she knew.

Though not hurt himself, the driver of the vehicle had been badly shaken up. So had Sarah's boyfriend, Michael. He'd been in here this morning, apparently, but wasn't in evidence now. Sarah's spleen had been removed in surgery before dawn. Greg Snow had been one of the surgeons involved. Sarah had come back from Recovery at mid-morning.

Now she was alert enough to raise a pale smile at Caitlin's humour, and had been downgraded to half-hourly observations, which was good. When Caitlin had checked her half an hour earlier, her blood pressure had been good at 115 over 75, and her pulse satisfactory as well.

Her liver should repair itself, and as for her lost spleen... Well, most people who'd had them removed seemed to manage very well without them. No one was fully certain what the spleen actually did. Medical scientists had determined that it acted as an extra filter in the body, and that it had some influence on the immune system as well, but in both cases it wasn't the major organ involved.

Rarely, a missing spleen could lead to some problems with the blood or immune systems, but it wasn't likely. The bottom line was that Sarah had been lucky, and she knew it.

'Glad you're here, Caitlin,' she murmured through dry lips. 'I keep getting flashbacks to that car coming at me out of nowhere... If I hadn't been yelling at Michael...'

'Don't talk about it yet,' Caitlin urged her. 'Just rest, OK? Would you like some ice?'

'Yes, please!'

'Just a minute, then.'

Caitlin was very aware that Angus had just entered the room. They nodded briefly at each other, and their gazes locked for one smouldering second before she darted hers away. She was already hot and happy and jittery inside, and didn't want to feel any of that in her work environment.

She knew Angus was here to give Mrs Lyristakis another update on her boys. The anxious mother still hadn't seen them, having developed a fever which was giving cause for concern.

Caitlin and Angus had had their dinner together last night at seven, after her working day had ended at three. He'd taken her to a Turkish restaurant, with low, smoky lighting and exotic music and they'd just talked for three hours about so many things. It kept coming back to her today—little insights into how he thought and felt, a clever or quirky turn of phrase, things they agreed on and things they didn't.

He'd seemed to like it when she hadn't agreed with him, and had challenged her about it with a wicked glint in his eye. Then he'd goaded her into such a spirited defence of her views that they'd soon both been laughing and light-heartedly shouting each other down.

Dropping her home again, he hadn't kissed her. Which was good. Only she ached for it so badly even now that it was a relief to be able to leave the room in search of Sarah's cup of ice chips.

Returning a minute later, Caitlin was due once more to take Sarah's observations. Pulse up over eighty now. Close to ninety, in fact. That wasn't good. Was it just because Sarah had been thinking about the accident and her argument with Michael?

Fitting the blood pressure cuff in place, Caitlin found that this measurement, too, was less satisfactory than it had been half an hour ago. One-ten over sixty-five.

Angus was about to leave so she grabbed his attention with the quick use of his name, not sure if she was reacting too soon to what could easily be a temporary fluctuation in those vital signs. He turned, and just the sight of his dark, serious gaze was enough to make her heart jump.

'What's up?' he asked in an off-hand, professional tone.

Not for the first time, she marvelled at the contrast between his formality and professional air in this environment and the man she was getting to know elsewhere. It shouldn't have been the sexiest phenomenon she'd ever experienced, but somehow it was, something secret and special that anchored her and had her soaring at the same time.

'Um, this patient's obs. Pulse is up and blood pressure's down,' she summarised quickly, disturbed at the direction of her thoughts.

Sarah had her eyes closed now.

'She's about twelve hours post-op,' Caitlin went on. 'Splenectomy and some liver damage. She's a nurse on the gynae ward, by the way. Sarah McNulty. I know she's not your patient, but would you mind having a look since you're here?'

'Sure.' He nodded, following her to the bedside. 'Let me cross-check those obs, then. Sarah, I'm going to take your pulse again, OK? Caitlin, did you check her drainage tube?'

'Not yet. I'll do it now.'

She lifted the sheet and found that Sarah's movements had kinked the tube.

'Pulse *is* raised,' Angus agreed, then added a telling, 'Hmm!' He'd seen what had happened when Caitlin straightened the tube.

Caitlin saw it, too. A small surge of frank blood, where before there had been only the expected pale pink discharge. He turned to Sarah again. She'd opened her eyes now, more alert and, with her own professional experience, a little suspicious.

'Looks like I'm going to have to prod you a bit,' Angus told her. 'What rate is her drip flowing at, by the way, Caitlin?'

She told him.

'And how much are we getting at the other end?'

She checked the bag, and reached the same result that he did. Urine output was less than it should be, given the fluid that was going in through the drip.

Meanwhile, Angus was palpating Sarah's abdomen and firing careful questions at her. 'How's this? Tender? Obviously it is, because of the surgery, but how about here? Now, here?'

Half a minute later, he took Caitlin aside and said, 'There's blood gathering internally in her abdomen, pooling to either side as you'd expect since she's lying flat. And you saw what was coming into the tube. I'd say there's a liver gusher, but how serious it's hard to say. I notice Greg Snow's been seeing her post-op. Is he around?'

'He should be, I think. Somewhere in the hospital, anyway. He was in earlier, of course.'

'Better page him. I'll wait, if you like. I have some phone calls I can make from the desk.'

Greg turned up within three minutes and assessed the situation for himself, with both Angus and Caitlin looking on and Sarah alert enough to be concerned as well. They knew each other slightly, Greg and Sarah, through mutual medical friends here.

Which was perhaps why Greg at first tried to play the thing down. 'Yes, there's a bit of a bleed, Sarah,' he said, 'but what we'll do is put up some blood and keep a close eye on things overnight, OK?'

Caitlin saw Angus shift uneasily, and knew he disagreed.

Greg hadn't picked up on it. 'Thanks, Dr Ferguson,' he said, quite relaxed as he moved towards the doorway. 'And…' he checked Caitlin's name badge quickly, '…Caitlin, too. Sorry.' He gave a naughty-boy grin. Caitlin found it the reverse of charming. 'But if you'd come out with me some time, I'd get a better handle on your name.'

'It's not a problem, Dr Snow,' she said smoothly. 'There's nothing of mine you need to have a handle on, as far as I'm concerned.'

He chose to treat the line as a flirtation unfortunately, and gave a caressing laugh.

Angus had witnessed the whole exchange and was frowning darkly and bristling at Greg now.

'Hang on a tick,' he said. He put a hand on Greg's elbow and guided him into the corridor. 'Don't you think…?'

Caitlin didn't hear the rest. She'd turned back to Sarah, who managed weakly, 'It's OK, then?'

'Yes, seems to be.'

'Can I have some more ice?'

'Here, can you reach it yourself?'

'If I could have the bed a bit higher…'

Caitlin raised it several inches, Sarah reached for the ice…and there was another gush of crimson blood into the abdominal drainage tube.

'Dr Snow?' Caitlin called, and raced out of the room. 'I think the situation's getting worse…'

'I'll leave you to it, Greg,' Angus said, and strode off down the corridor. He didn't find time for a special glance or a smile at Caitlin, and she was appalled at how much she minded.

Greg came back to Sarah, went through everything again and fifteen minutes later she was on her way back down to surgery.

'So, which is it to be?' Angus said to Caitlin over the phone late on Tuesday afternoon, after she'd had a quiet day off. 'A Hollywood blockbuster or a quirky foreign flick?'

On Monday night he'd taken her to a concert at the Opera House, such an utterly safe sort of evening that at one point she'd accused him of teasing her. 'I keep expecting to look over my shoulder and find you've hired a chaperone, Angus!'

They'd arrived in separate taxis and shared one as far as her place on the way home. She'd then tried to make a show of independence by paying half, which had been such a distraction that they hadn't even kissed. And at the concert itself there had scarcely been the opportunity for wayward behaviour.

Yet it had been so indescribably nice just to sit silently next to him, with the music washing over her, aware of exactly how his limbs angled and fell, able to feel the faint warmth of his body against her bare shoulder and smell the subtle, nutty scent of his aftershave.

For such a safe, chaste and formal evening, it had definitely left its mark. And as they'd shuffled their way out of the concert hall amongst the press of people when it was all over, he'd said casually, 'So…a movie tomorrow?'

And now, as promised, he was on the phone with the cinema listings from today's newspaper at the ready.

It took them several minutes to consider the options, and they ended up choosing something very light and commercial that was showing in the city, finishing early enough to permit supper afterwards.

Movies turned out to be more dangerous than concerts. Cinemas were dark, for a start, and they were sitting in the back row. Choosing a romantic comedy, in hindsight, had been a mistake, too. In romantic comedies people kissed, and highly paid American film stars generated such convincing chemistry in their on-screen relationships that you began to believe they deserved their multi-million dollar contracts.

And chemistry could be catching. When Angus slid his arm around Caitlin's shoulder she left it there, and when he turned her face to his to kiss her she completely lost track of the plot of the film.

Afterwards, they drove up to Oxford Street for supper at an impossibly fashionable café where their waitress, Bialle, as she'd introduced herself in ominous tones, was so frighteningly macabre in her dress and manner that she reduced both Angus and Caitlin to fits of guilty laughter.

'I expect her poems are going badly,' Angus suggested with exaggerated sympathy after Bialle had stalked off with their order.

'Or her performance art,' Caitlin supplied. 'Did you see the look she gave me when I ordered the strawberry pavlova?'

'Admit it, it's not the hip dessert for the next millennium, Caitlin.'

'So they shouldn't have it on the menu!'

'But it's a test, you see. Anyone who orders it is immediately branded as so uncool that no member of the serving staff is obliged to take any notice of them from then on, and can thereby save their best efforts for any passing celebrities or junior media moguls.'

'Ah, thank you for pointing that out. Do you mind that you're out with a woman who's so far from the forefront of culinary fashion?'

'It depends. If Bialle favours me with the same black look she gave you, I may be forced to disown you out of sheer self-preservation.'

They joked their way through supper, back to his car and then home to her place, and tonight he didn't give her the chance to get flustered and stubborn over issues of independence, he just took her in his arms and kissed her so deeply and lengthily and thoroughly and wonderfully that she was weak in every limb, tingling in every pore and swollen and aching in places she hardly had names for.

If he'd suggested coming upstairs, she couldn't have found the word 'no' anywhere in her vocabulary, but he didn't suggest it, just let her go, finally, with a light kiss on her nose and a whispered, 'Goodnight.'

She hesitated for endless seconds before she managed to say the word back to him.

'We've missed you, Caitlin,' Josie Wade said on Wednesday morning.

'I've only been off for one day!'

'I know, but Mrs Lyristakis likes you, and her infection was proving very nasty, which means she hasn't been allowed down to see her kids, so she's been pretty low. And Mrs Best was sorry she missed saying goodbye—in fact, she'll pop in, I expect, because of course she's still down on the fifth floor with William a lot. Mrs Reid was afraid *she'd* miss seeing you, too.'

'Oh, she's not being discharged already?'

'To Newby House,' Josie said quietly, naming the hospice in Clovelly with its magnificent views of the ocean. 'She's going down fast. You'll notice a change. She'd like to go home, but her pain management is so poor now that she agreed the hospice was best. What's more, she has absolutely no appetite and we're not forcing the issue.'

'It's happening more quickly than we thought, then.'

'Yes, her doctors at first said she'd have several weeks, but I don't see it now.'

'How's Stevie?'

'She's adjusting…as much as anyone can. The option of Newby House shocked her at first. Meanwhile, Sarah's doing a lot better physically, but seems pretty low in spirits. Her boyfriend hasn't been in to see her so maybe that's the problem. If you get time to talk to her…'

'As usual, that's a big if!'

'I know.'

'And the Lyristakis boys?'

'One's out of danger and doing fine. The other…goes from crisis to crisis, but the tide may have turned now. Dr Ferguson and Dr Hunterdon have agreed that Mrs Lyristakis can see both boys today at last, and they'd like you to go down, too. She's been rotten physically, as I said, and *very* emotional at times. If you can find a way to stop that from happening in front of the boys, it would be good.'

'Find a way? I'll just tell her straight out,' Caitlin said firmly, her own direct nature coming to the fore. 'It'll make sense to her, I'm sure, that if she's sobbing they'll get more alarmed about their own recovery and that could well set them back.'

'Yes, it's a good theory, Caitlin, but…'

The planned trip to PICU was scheduled for later in the morning after Angus had finished his surgical list for the day. With Christmas and New Year over, the hospital was immediately gearing up to the maximum for elective and non-urgent procedures again, and their own ward would receive several new pre-op and post-op patients this morning. Also, there was Mrs Reid's transfer to Newby House to attend to.

The palliative care team had been brought in several days

ago to take over responsibility for Mrs Reid's medication so Caitlin had nothing to do in that area but check that her dose this morning was timed to make the ambulance transfer as comfortable as possible. She then needed to get on the phone to Newby House with the expected time of arrival, make sure that Mrs Reid had all her belongings, help with the transfer from bed to ambulance and ease Stevie's concern by answering her questions.

Everything was managed according to plan, and Betty Reid was alert enough as she left to thank everyone on 6A for their care and support. Inevitably, though, her medication would need to become heavier and she would probably lapse into a state of drowsy passivity for the last phase of her life. That didn't mean that Stevie's presence would be unimportant to her, even when she was no longer able to acknowledge it with words. Caitlin knew that it would be a very poignant time for Betty's daughter.

Sarah was down to four-hourly observations after her second bout of surgery, her pain was much less severe and she would be discharged early next week. The fact didn't seem to have much power to cheer her up.

'How's Michael?' Caitlin asked as she checked the wound site and took Sarah's blood pressure, temperature and pulse.

Sarah's face twisted. 'We've split up,' she said. 'Those two times he came in after the accident were just duty calls, and we both knew it. We weren't right together. It's for the best.'

'Still, you don't sound too happy about it.'

Sarah moved restlessly. 'Oh...'. I've been so stupid, that's all. Not a fun realisation. Strange, I was just so intoxicated by Michael at first. He seemed so...so *big city* and exciting—you know, with his job in advertising—and I felt like I'd really *arrived*, like I was going to be someone better just by being in his world. But that's so stupid. When you're with someone it has to be because you can be who you *are*, not who you think you want to be. Remember that guy Pete?'

'The vet science student? The one you were going out with before Michael?'

'The one I ditched the moment Michael showed an interest, you mean?' Sarah countered in a tone of bitter self-reproach.

'Is that how it happened?'

'Yes! And it was inexcusable. No wonder he hasn't tried to get in touch. I gave him that line about ''wanting to be friends''. Of course I didn't mean it then, and he knew that, and of course he's got too much pride to take second-best like that! But if he walked through this door right now, I'd…' Her eyes misted and she choked back a sob. 'Sorry, I'm just feeling sorry for myself because I've been such a fool. You've got work to do. How's my temp and BP?'

'Fine,' Caitlin said, and gave her the figures. 'But you're obviously not.'

'I'll be OK. Go, Caitie-pie. Remorse is not a pretty sight, is it?' She smiled weakly and once more shooed Caitlin from the room.

Caitlin left, quite worried about her friend and wondering if there was anything she could do to help. As she didn't know Pete, it didn't seem likely.

At eleven she was ready to prepare Mrs Lyristakis for her visit to PICU. She wanted to change her nightgown and do her hair, and needed a new dressing on her surgical site as well. She was nervous and tearful already, and Mr Lyristakis was obviously dreading the whole thing.

'I've tried to tell her,' he muttered to Caitlin. 'Nico will at least be able to smile at her, but Alex…' He shook his head, then quickly fumbled for a large white handkerchief and blew his nose. 'My big, strong Alex is so ill…so ill!'

Caitlin told her patient about the importance of not frightening Alex or Nico by the degree of her own emotion, but it was already obvious that it was going to be a struggle. They had arranged to meet the two surgeons at the entrance to PICU, but Dr Hunterdon and Dr Ferguson had evidently conferred on the subject and changed their minds because now, at the last minute, here they were, stepping quietly into her room together.

Caitlin's heart started fluttering straight away, and a word that Sarah had used popped unbidden into her head. Intoxicated.

On paper, I've done just what Sarah is punishing herself over, she realised. I ditched Scott the moment Angus showed an interest. Only it didn't feel like that. It *wasn't* like that! Was it?

Angus found a moment to send her a quick, private smile, with shared memories of last night smoking deep in his eyes, but she couldn't respond to it. He was leaving in four days, and they'd known each other less than two weeks. It was just one short week since she'd given Scott back his ring.

And last night she'd gone to that movie and supper with Angus and had come so close to inviting him up to her flat that she'd actually dreamed of him being with her in her bed afterwards—wild, sensual, climactic dreams all night long, of his hot body on hers and his lips tasting her skin which made her blush as she thought of them.

She fought the memories off and greeted Ralph Hunterdon, too disturbed about Angus to look at him now at all.

Dr Hunterdon was a bluff and somewhat weather-beaten man of about fifty, totally devoted to his work and almost incapable of conversation with anyone who wasn't a surgeon. He'd developed a passable bedside manner despite this handicap, however, and replaced words with heartfelt pats of reassurance on shoulders and hands whenever he could, leaving any explanations in lay language to his junior colleagues.

Angus Ferguson, however, had no need to resort to body language. 'We thought it best to meet you here, Mrs Lyristakis,' he said at once, 'because I've realised I should explain to you once again just what you'll see with Alex and Nico.'

'All right.' The response was shaky.

'Firstly, Alex won't be able to speak to you. He's still on a respirator, which means there's a tube down his throat that can be very uncomfortable. Also, he may be asleep as he's pretty heavily medicated to ward off pain, but I do want and need you to talk to him because the encouragement that will give him is very valuable.'

How clever he is, Caitlin realised. He's phrasing it in such a positive way. I should have done that. Instead, because I thought it was so important, I ended up almost bullying her.

'Now, Nico,' he was saying, 'probably will be awake. He's very eager to see you and is a little worried that we haven't told him the truth about how well you're getting on so, again, show him that you're going to be fine, despite the way you're trussed up and confined.'

Fotini Lyristakis nodded, big-eyed and much, much calmer.

'Thanks, Angus,' Caitlin told him as they walked down the corridor in the wake of Mrs Lyristakis's trolley, an orderly, Mr Lyristakis and Dr Hunterdon.

She hadn't wanted to connect with him on a personal level, but this was more about work, and she felt she had to.

'What for?' he asked.

'For getting Mrs L. so calm and focused. I hadn't tackled the issue nearly so well.'

'But you couldn't have,' he pointed out with some truth. 'You hadn't seen the boys.' Then, in a lower tone, he asked 'Are you always so hard on yourself, Caitlin?'

'I'm not hard on myself.'

'Yes, you are. I can see quite clearly that you're punishing yourself for last night. For the fact that we so nearly—'

'OK,' she agreed. 'Please, let's not talk about it now!'

'Hardly the time, is it?' he agreed calmly.

He touched her lightly in the small of her back as they waited at the large lift, and it was too much like a caress.

There was something very intimate about the snatched moment. Dr Hunterdon was flipping through some notes, and Angus and Caitlin had dropped to the back of the little group. To all intents and purposes, they were alone, but then Dr Hunterdon shut his folder and they reached the open lift. Entering it, she could feel Angus's attention fixed on her like radiant heat, but quite obviously the chance for private conversation had ended.

Which was good. She couldn't say it all now. She needed time. Time to find the courage to say it at all for a start. And the time to say it properly. Angus at least deserved *that*.

Meanwhile, she *didn't* need to be aware of him like this. It was hardly helpful when awareness co-existed with Sarah McNulty's words drumming over and over in her head.

Intoxicated. Inexcusable. Stupid.

With the lift doors closed, Mr and Mrs Lyristakis were fully focused on each other, the orderly was struggling to get Mrs Lyristakis's trolley wheels to behave as they should and Dr Hunterdon was talking surgery incomprehensibly to Angus. Only Caitlin's attention was free and it fixed on the dynamic, impossible man as if drawn there like a magnet.

She was intensely conscious of the masculine contour of his body so close to hers in the confined space, and if there had been any possibility of moving away from him she would have done so. He shifted on his feet at that moment, as if uncomfortable in his own skin, and she was sure he had picked up on exactly what she was feeling. If he'd guessed, would that make it easier?

They were at the fourth floor at last, and now that there was freedom of movement she went and walked by the orderly, Adam, who she knew well enough to chat to. Dr Hunterdon would probably be grateful to be able to monopolise Angus's attention, and Angus himself would breathe a sigh of relief, too. He'd wanted the two of them to see as much as possible of each other this week but to see each other in this sort of situation was worse than not seeing each other at all.

The paediatric intensive care unit was a quiet, frighteningly technological place and contained some very sick children indeed. Alex and Nico were in adjoining cubicles but couldn't see each other. It had been easier, though, with this arrangement for Vasilios Lyristakis to spend vital time with each of his sons.

'Let's say hi to Alex first,' Angus suggested, and Mrs Lyristakis held herself together well as she spoke to the twelve-year-old and squeezed his hand, stretching awkwardly from her own confined position with her pelvis tightly girdled and her pinned leg immobilised. To facilitate her contact with Alex, one of her bed-rails was removed and this made things easier. Caitlin took it and propped it against the cubicle wall to get it out of the way.

Alex had been asleep, but now his eyes drifted open and he actually attempted a smile.

'Doesn't he look great, Fotini?' Vasilios enthused. And to him it was the truth after the way he'd seen his son a few days ago. A smile was a major milestone. For Mrs Lyristakis, though…

Her face worked and she turned to Angus. 'How long can I stay?'

'Well, let's see Nico now, and then I'll answer any questions you have, and you can come back in here. I hope you'll soon be able to spend as much time as you like with them, but I have to defer to Dr Hunterdon and Dr Webber—' the latter was the orthopaedic surgeon who had repaired her fractured pelvis and femur '—on the issue of your own condition.'

'I'm fine. There's nothing wrong with me. I'm perfectly well,' Mrs Lyristakis insisted extravagantly. It was an assertion that clearly offended Ralph Hunterdon's nose for accuracy, but Caitlin knew what she meant— Fotini wasn't going to let her own condition keep her away from her children any longer if she could possibly help it. Now she suppressed her emotion once again and said to Alex, 'We're going to see Nico, now, angel-face, and then we'll come back, OK?'

Oddly enough it was Nico, less seriously injured, who made Mrs Lyristakis crack. Perhaps it was because he was the younger of the two. Perhaps it was the size of his smile. Or perhaps it was the fact that immediately after the smile he burst very loudly into tears.

Whatever the reason, Mrs Lyristakis simply forgot that she was confined as if on a medieval rack by her pinned femur, forgot that her bed-rail had been removed and stretched so desperately across to her son that she slipped from the bed and onto the shiny floor. Her own scream of pain was drowned by a frantic yelp of dismay from Caitlin and shouts of horror from both doctors and Mr Lyristakis.

Nico screamed for his mother and she made a heroic attempt to reassure him. 'It's…all right, Nico. I'm…all right. Tell him, Vasilios!'

Vasilios turned his attention to his horrified son.

'Where's Webber?' Dr Hunterdon barked to Angus at the same time. 'Is it any use paging him? He's probably not even in the hospital.'

'Let's get her back in bed first and then worry about that,' Angus said. 'Adam, get yourself in here *now*!'

The orderly came running, as did a PICU nurse in his wake, her eyes wide and questioning.

Fotini was white with pain and moaning now.

'Oh…oh…oh…' she said, the sound rhythmic and continuous, and she was shaking with shock.

'Can the four of us manage it?' Angus speculated aloud. 'I think so! Let's not waste time!' He directed everyone into position in the space of seconds, then said, 'On three… One, two, three, and *up*!' then she was safely where she belonged again.

The crisis wasn't over, however. 'OK, good,' Angus went on. 'Now…I did an orthopaedics term about eight years ago…'

'As long as her pins haven't come out,' Dr Hunterdon came in, with doom in his voice. Phillippa Kirk, the PICU nurse, hissed with horror at the idea.

Angus examined them and pronounced them still in place, though they'd get Dr Webber in as soon as they could to make quite sure.

Then he adjusted her position so that her acute pain subsided to a nagging but bearable level. 'Is that better now?' He placed a hand on her shoulder.

'Much, yes! I cannot believe I did that!'

'None of us can,' he replied. 'It was practically superhuman!'

Dr Hunterdon grunted his agreement.

'We'll get her down to X-Ray straight away, though,' Angus told the medical personnel in an undertone. 'Webber will be cruising for blood if he decides we didn't take this seriously enough.'

Aloud, he explained the situation to Mr and Mrs Lyristakis and reassured Nico as well.

'I'll get on the phone to Radiology now and tell them to expect her,' Phillippa said.

'Adam, you'll take her down,' Angus told the orderly with casual authority.

'Before she goes to Radiology, though, there's some discharge from her surgical site,' Caitlin pointed out quietly to Angus now. 'Look, you can see the fresh discoloration seeping through the dressing.'

'Yes,' he agreed. 'You're right, Caitlin.' There came a phantom touch of approval against the small of her back and she flinched. Had he seen? 'Ralph? It could well have opened up, couldn't it?' he was saying to the older man.

Dr Hunterdon's beeper went at that moment, dividing his attention. 'I know what this'll be,' he said, 'and I'd better deal with it. Yes, do check it, Sister Gray.' He left the room.

Angus turned back to their patient. 'Mrs Lyristakis, you

heard that, didn't you? We're just going to check your incision, OK? Let us know if it feels unusually tender, won't you? Were you aware of any pain there as you fell?'

'Nothing I could feel beyond what was happening in my hips and leg,' she answered.

'And now?'

'It feels OK.'

'We'll check, though, just to make sure.'

He let Caitlin peel back the gauze pad that covered the place where the punctured bladder had been repaired, then examined the skin beneath as she was doing. They were so close that she could feel the sweep of hair across his forehead lightly brushing her cheek, and wished heartily that her awareness of him didn't feel so treacherously good.

The site of Mrs Lyristakis's incision had obviously been strained, as it looked redder than it should and was weeping freshly, but the stitches themselves were intact. 'Keep an eye on it, though,' Angus advised her as he straightened, 'over the next day or so.'

'Radiology is expecting her within the next few minutes,' Phillippa Kirk reported from the doorway.

'OK, good.' Angus nodded. 'Nico, we're going to take your mum away again for a bit to give her an X-ray, and then she can come back, all right?'

'Can Dad stay?'

'Sure... Mr Lyristakis?'

'I'll stay, Nico.'

'I must be off,' Ralph Hunterdon said, making a brief reappearance. 'Something's come up, and I'll already be late for my office hours.'

'I must head off, too,' Angus came in. 'Well handled, everyone, thank you. I'll let Dr Webber know about the X-ray so he can follow it up. Nico, you look after your mother from now on, and don't let her try any more cartwheels till at least next week, OK?'

Caitlin smiled unwillingly. She loved his sense of humour, familiar to her now. She didn't intend Angus to see the smile, but he did, and before she knew it their eyes had met and locked and they exchanged a moment of shared understanding...shared wanting...that made her miserable again.

She looked away at once, but he touched her on the shoulder. The Lyristakises were talking to Nico again. Adam had gone out to the nurses' station to make a phone call to his supervisor, and Dr Hunterdon was already on his way out of the unit.

'We didn't get a chance to finish what we were talking about earlier,' he told her.

'I know,' she said tightly, 'but we can't talk about it now. Can we meet?'

'I want to. What are your hours?'

'Evenings tomorrow, Friday and Saturday.'

'I'm in surgery tomorrow and Friday from six in the morning onwards, and I have a thousand things to do before Sunday.'

'Tonight?'

'I have a dinner meeting with Michael Bowen to get me up to speed on the set-up in Los Angeles. He's very frustrated at missing the opportunity, but with both arms in plaster it's out of the question for him. I've promised to foster our professional contacts there as much as I can so that he may get the chance to go himself some time in the future, and he wants to give me as much detail as possible on what he knows already about their way of working. We'll be talking half the night, I expect. I could come around to your flat afterwards on my way home and—'

'No!' The last thing she wanted was to meet him on the dangerous ground of her flat late at night. And anyway... 'If you've got surgery at six the next morning, after a heavy evening of work, it's an impossible time to talk.'

'I know.' He nodded tersely. 'But that means Saturday morning is our first chance.'

'Saturday morning would be fine, Angus,' she told him heavily. In fact, she had begun to realise, the closer to his departure their next private meeting together, the better.

CHAPTER NINE

THE phone rang at nine o'clock on Saturday morning and Caitlin was breathless even before she picked it up, certain that it would be Angus, suggesting a change of plan. He was supposed to be coming round at ten, and she was dreading it.

But it wasn't Angus's voice, although the deep, teasing tones went unidentified for several seconds as she frantically tried to put a name to them. Finally, she did.

'Scott!'

He gave a theatrical sigh. 'How quickly they forget!'

'Scott, I—'

'Listen, I'm settled in to my new place now, and I'd like to come and pick up my stereo. How would eleven o'clock be?'

'Um, fine, I suppose.' Angus would be gone by then. He'd better be! 'Although Erin is driving up from Canberra in a rental van today—she starts back at work in the maternity unit on Monday—and I promised to help her unload over lunch. She's going to be sharing a place with a couple of nurses.'

'Busy day!'

If only he knew!

'So I can't hang about if you're late is what I'm saying,' she pressed on.

'I won't be,' he promised breezily, although he certainly couldn't claim obsessive punctuality as a personal fault.

In the past she'd pointed out to him more than once that detouring to buy flowers as an apology for being late had the predictable side-effect of making him later still. Not that any self-respecting female begrudged a gift of flowers...

Angus brought some, a glorious bunch of warm summer

colour. The gesture churned her up more than ever and stopping to buy them hadn't even made him late. Her bedside clock read one minute past ten.

'Angus, you didn't have to.'

'It was an impulse.'

'These are… These are…' She felt their cool petals tickle her nose.

'Going to wilt if you don't put them in a vase straight away,' he teased gently. 'It's going to be hot again.'

'Yes. A vase,' she said vaguely, and found the only one she owned, high in a top cupboard, unused since Scott's last apology months ago.

'Now you're supposed to offer me coffee,' he suggested helpfully, when her unsteady hands had heaped the flowers into the water-filled vase.

'No… I *can't*!'

'Caitlin, what's wrong? What's this ''talk'' about?' Angus urged.

In his heart, of course, he already knew. Her open face and her steadfast blue eyes were so easy to read.

But he let her say it.

'I can't spend any more time with you.' She was trembling, and already starting to cry wildly. 'You're going away on Sunday. For months. And I've known you for two weeks.'

'And I love you,' he said quietly, pulling her into his arms.

'You *can't*! I don't want you to!' She fought him, twisting her shoulders and pulling her face away.

'Why not?'

'Because then you'll think you have the right to ask the same of me. And how can I know? How can I say yes to that yet?'

'You *do* know,' he urged.

They were both losing control. He could feel it. Winding his arms more tightly around her, loving the willowy strength and suppleness of her form, he could feel the helpless response in her. She wasn't fighting him. Maybe she wanted to, but her body was more in touch with the truth than her mind.

'I don't!' she insisted.

'I'll believe you if you can say it without shaking,' he whispered, tasting her neck and her earlobe, trailing his mouth very slowly and deliberately across to claim her lips. 'If you can say it without sighing against my lips… If you can say it without that little sound escaping from your throat…'

Caitlin couldn't. She didn't even try. Instead, she surrendered helplessly to the exquisite torture of being in his arms. Oh, yes, *that* part had never been in doubt. Her body responded to his like the strings of a violin vibrating to the draw of a bow, and had done so from the beginning. She could have run her fingers over his face, pressed herself against him, length to length, pulled at his clothes in order to get to the hot satin of his skin.

In that sense, he intoxicated her. She knew that. But at the moment that was the only thing she trusted about what she knew.

Breaking away from him and hugging her arms around herself in a defensive gesture, she demanded, 'What are you asking of me, Angus? You're going away in less than two days, so how can it matter to you if I'm making this pathetic attempt to hold you off by saying I can't see you? I won't be *able* to see you after tomorrow and then the whole thing will come to an end.

'Four months is a long time, and the Pacific Ocean is a lot wider than the distance between Canberra and Newcastle. Scott and I didn't survive that distance. You and I won't survive this one. Not at this stage, when we've only just met. What does it matter if it ends now or tomorrow? So what do you want?'

'Commitment,' he said.

'*What?*'

'I want us to make a commitment to each other,' he answered simply. 'I want us to say, out loud, looking into each other's eyes, that we love each other and we're going to wait for each other, that we're *not* going to let four months and several thousand miles get in the way. I want us to agree in actual out-loud *words* that this is too deep and too good to risk letting go of. This fellowship in Los Angeles is too important for me to handle it in a state of miserable uncertainty. Not just important for me and my own career, but for the hospital and what we hope to achieve here.

'I can't afford to be distracted, wondering what you're doing back here, wondering if there's another man waiting for you, capturing your heart as soon as you feel it's free, feeling our two weeks fade and knowing it's fading for you, too, so you'll start to doubt that it had any reality at all. We have to seize hold of it now when it's fresh and we *know* it's real.'

'But—'

'Say you'll marry me, Caitlin, when I get back. I need that certainty.'

'No!' She stepped back, shaking her head frantically. 'Angus, ten days ago I was engaged to someone else.'

'It takes courage to admit to a mistake and act on it,' he urged. 'You did that. You can do this.'

He was relentless. His dark eyes were glittering, his shoulders were hunched with tension, the planes of his face were stark and uncompromising and he was as restless as she was in the way he moved around her cramped little flat. And he was totally unfair.

'How can you call it courage?' she stormed. 'That makes me a coward if I say no.'

'I didn't mean that—'

She ignored him. 'And I'm *not* a coward! You know what I feel about this! I don't want to hurt Scott by acting in any way that denies any value in what we had.'

'Your heart was free when you and I met. You know that now. You just hadn't realised it at the time.'

'But from his perspective it would have to feel like a betrayal, almost as hurtful as if you and I had actually had an affair. I once thought I loved him enough to marry him. I won't be faithless to that.'

'So your answer is no.'

'It has to be, Angus.' She was crying again. 'And perhaps you're right. I don't have the courage. The courage to trust what I feel.'

There was a short silence, then he said slowly, 'Would it help, do you think, if you could separate out the two strands of it?'

'What do you mean?'

He paced to her kitchen doorway, then turned and came towards her again. 'I'm hearing two things from you, Caitlin.' He made two tight, white fists in the air. 'That you don't trust what you feel, and that you don't want to betray what you had with Scott.'

'Yes…'

'If somehow I could take one of those strands of feeling away…'

'How can you *make* me trust what I feel?'

His gaze locked with hers, dark, caressing and powerful. 'I could,' he said. 'I know I could, but that's not the strand I was thinking of.'

'Explain, Angus,' she demanded wearily.

This time the silence was much longer. When Angus spoke at last the words seemed to drag from him and his mouth was twisted as if it disgusted him to feel them there. 'What makes you so sure,' he said heavily, 'that Scott was faithful to *you*?'

His meaning was quite clear, and Caitlin's response was instinctive. 'I don't believe you! You're insinuating—'

'All those nights and weekends when you were in Canberra or Sydney and he was in Newcastle…'

'No! It's too convenient, Angus. Don't—don't make me

distrust you!' The possibility hurt badly. She *had* trusted him until now.

'I saw him myself, right there in my lecture before Christmas, with a third year medical student,' he was saying steadily. 'A redhead.'

'Yet somehow this is the first time you've seen fit to mention it?'

'Yes,' he agreed on a sigh, ignoring the icy sarcasm in her tone. 'Believe me, I've been struggling with the issue. And it was probably a mistake even now.'

'Oh, definitely!' She laughed harshly. 'Next time try a different strategy. This one didn't work.'

'Caitlin, I didn't want to hurt you, that was all.' He tried to touch her, but she wouldn't let him, although she hoped he didn't guess what it cost her to push away those warm, strong arms as they came to her shoulders. 'I've been racked about this from the moment I met Scott at your parents' place. I only told you now because—'

'You'd run out of other weapons,' she finished for him.

'Yes,' he agreed simply. 'I had. I have. But it's no good, is it? It's over.'

'It never started, Angus.'

'It could have,' he insisted. 'It *would* have!'

'Perhaps.' She nodded. 'Except I can't see that. There's too much in the way. And I despise you for trying to make mileage out of something you saw in a lecture. You must have misunderstood. Of course Scott had female friends in Newcastle. I've met some of them myself. But to fling it at me like that as a way of persuading me to give myself to you…'

'Put like that, it sounds so ugly.'

'Because it is.'

'No! You *know* I didn't want it this way!'

'Didn't you? You—you'd better leave, I think.'

He nodded. 'You're right. It does seem like the only thing left to do.'

His mouth snapped shut and his tightly pressed lips were a harsh line across his face. Neither of them said goodbye.

When he'd gone, she flung herself onto the bed and cried for the hopeless mess of it all, for what might have been and for the suffering she'd seen in Angus's dark face... Cried, until she remembered that Scott was due soon, and he mustn't see her like this. By noon, however, he hadn't turned up, and when her doorbell sounded it was Erin standing there.

They spent two hours unloading the rental van and arranging Erin's things in the three-bedroomed shared house in Sydenham. Erin was starting to seem a little more like her old self after her washed-out state over Christmas. Caitlin wasn't fooled, though. Perhaps because she, too, was hiding inner turmoil beneath an outward veneer of competence and humour.

When they were seated in the elderly yet spacious kitchen of Erin's new house with a cup of tea, Caitlin demanded finally, 'Are you *ever* going to tell me about this bloke of yours, Erin?'

Erin sighed, and scraped some blonde hair back from her face. 'He was never mine,' she answered. 'That was the problem. He was engaged to someone else.'

'And you got in that deep? Just wanting him from a distance?'

'We were good friends,' Erin said. 'Then something started to happen. He knew it. He felt it too. Just in the space of one night. We...almost...went to bed together. Then he said he couldn't, and I felt the same. It wasn't right. He had to break it off with his fiancée first. Only that never happened. He didn't phone. He obviously changed his mind.'

'Are you sure, though?'

'Caitlin, I was at their wedding! I had to sit through it, watching how tense they both looked, knowing, *feeling* it was wrong but watching them go through with it. I guess he'd told her about me or something, and she hadn't quite forgiven him yet. After that I couldn't stand it. That's why I came back early. I left London while they were still on their honeymoon. But I was wrong. I should have stayed, at least long enough to confront him, find out the truth.'

'Do you think so?'

'That's what's killing me now. Not knowing *why*. If he was too scared. Or if he really loves her after all. Or if he doesn't love anybody! When it's messy like that, when you don't know, it just makes it so hard to move on!'

Caitlin couldn't find the words of comfort she wanted, just had to reach across the table and pat Erin's hand. Evidently it helped a little.

'Thanks,' Erin said. 'And I *will* move on! That's one thing about them actually being married. The spiked steel gates of matrimony have clanged shut. The drawbridge of domesticity has been raised. The soldiers of wedlock are standing guard.' She illustrated the drama-laden words with extravagant gestures, and finished, 'He's gone!'

'You're laughing again,' Caitlin observed. 'That's good.'

'It is. It feels good,' Erin agreed, stretching herself like a cat in the sun.

She'd always had an outrageous sense of humour. No subject was sacred enough to be safe from her wit, even her own damaged heart.

Eventually she'll be all right, Caitlin knew.

And so will I.

'But what about you?' Erin probed, pouring another cup of tea. 'You don't look happy yourself. Are you missing Scott more than you thought?'

'Missing the certainty,' Caitlin said. It was the only part of the truth that she could trust to words today.

* * *

Scott phoned her at work at four, casual in his apology and sketchy in his explanation about what had kept him.

'Sorry,' he said. 'I got held up. Could I drop in and get the key from you at work and get the stereo now? Then I'll drop the key back again.'

'You mean right now?'

'Right now,' he promised.

'OK…'

It would be good to see him…someone who grinned like a naughty boy when he was caught out in mischief, someone who shrugged off his own faults so that other people shrugged them off, too. Someone golden and confident and casual and— faithless?

He arrived as promised when she was at the nurses' station, and dropped a quick take-it-or-leave-it kiss on her lips. He had gone again in a moment with her key, promising to have it back "before you come off".

The shift dragged. Caitlin had too much on her mind, and nothing about today was helping. Even Sarah McNulty made things worse.

'This is Pete,' she said with a brilliant, loving smile when she introduced Caitlin to the tall chestnut-haired man who'd shown up for visiting hours.

'Pete.' Caitlin nodded, and understood everything just from the expression on her friend's face.

Did it tell her anything about her own situation, though? If it did, she was too confused to understand what.

She knew Angus wouldn't be here today. He was making the final preparations for going away, and his patients had already been taken over by another surgeon. He had no reason to come to 6A any more, anyway. Mrs Best had been discharged days ago, and Mrs Lyristakis had been moved to the orthopaedic ward now that her bladder repair was sufficiently healed.

What would it serve to see him, anyway?

She had yelled at him this morning, challenged his truth-fulness, questioned his motives and said no to his proposal of marriage. He'd laid himself on the line and she hadn't known how to meet him halfway. What red-blooded male would for-give all that?

Meanwhile, her dinner break passed, her shift drew to a close and Scott hadn't come back...

The phone call from Accident and Emergency came through for her at ten to eleven.

'Is this Caitlin Gray?' said the voice of an unknown nurse. 'We have Scott Sinclair down here, asking for you.'

'Asking for me?'

'He's been hurt. A head injury, and he's drifting in and out of consciousness. Can you come down as soon as you're fin-ished your shift?'

'Of course. Can you...tell me what happened?'

'He's been pretty hazy about it so far. Apparently he was carrying some hi-fi equipment—'

His stereo, Caitlin thought.

'From his car, and he was mugged by some addicts. They took his wallet as well. But, if you'll excuse me, we're pretty busy down here...'

'I'll be down as soon as I can,' she promised shakily.

There was no problem with getting off a few minutes early. Her patients tonight were stable and satisfactory after routine operations, and her night-shift counterpart, a very competent older woman called Doreen Mather, had already arrived.

Accident and Emergency *was* busy. An ambulance pulled in as Caitlin arrived, there was an emergency cardiac resus-citation team gathered and the nurse who'd phoned her was nowhere to be found. Nor was Scott at first. Caitlin finally found him in Cubicle Four, and heard a quick report from the nurse, Mee Yung Tan.

'They haven't decided what to do with him yet,' she ex-plained. 'His neuro signs are all good, but he's been swimming in and out of consciousness and they'll have to bandage his head pretty thoroughly. How long can you stay?'

'All night, if he wants me.'

'Let's wait and see,' Mee Yung said. 'Now... I've got to go.'

She packed up her equipment trolley and wheeled it out, and Caitlin went to the bedside, took Scott's hand and said softly, 'Hi...'

Scott half opened his eyes, winced, closed them again and said very weakly, 'I'm glad you've come. Don't go, will you? I really need you, Caitlin.'

It was exactly two weeks since his near-fatal brush with the blue-ringed octopus, and, as she had that day, Caitlin stayed with Scott for some hours.

First he was taken for a scan, which came out normal to everyone's relief. Caitlin then accompanied him up to 6B, though he hadn't opened his eyes or spoken a word since his earlier greeting. Medicated now, he seemed to be thoroughly asleep.

At three, dropping in her tracks, she finally decided to go home and to sleep herself, but only realised when she reached her flat that Scott still had her key. Resignedly, she turned around and went back to the hospital to collect it, exhausted and uncomfortable about being on the roads on her little motorbike this late at night.

She didn't get to bed, finally, until four. After sleeping restlessly until eight, she then felt too much on edge to go back to sleep so she had a shower, dressed casually in blue and beige floral shorts and a matching blouse, grabbed some juice, cereal and coffee and headed straight back to Southshore in the rising morning heat.

Angus would also be awake by now. He was leaving today. This afternoon. Her heart twisted.

Not that his departure should or could matter to her. She'd

given him her answer, and didn't see how it could have been any different.

Scott was feeling a lot better, but he had no appetite and was still reacting to Caitlin's presence in a needy and sentimental way.

'We threw a lot away last week, didn't we?' he said. 'Four years. Some good times. Some nice plans.'

'It was the right thing,' Caitlin answered him. About this, at least, she was sure.

Scott wasn't, though. 'Was it?' he said. '*Was* it, Caitlin?'

'You seemed quite breezy about it last week.'

'But this accident has really made me think.' He sighed. 'And question my values.'

'Don't, Scott,' she begged. 'You're too shaky and tired now to know what you want.'

'Even if it's what I wanted every minute for four years?' he challenged softly. '*You?*'

'Don't say that now!' She knew she had to stand firm, yet it was hard when he was so emotionally frail.

'So when should I say it?' he pressed. 'You're saying I'm not in full possession of myself, aren't you?'

'Well, *are* you?'

'Of course! Look, I can even appreciate Sister Buckley's fine figure as she bends over the next bed.'

He grinned wickedly and gestured over to Nurse Georgina Buckley who was taking another patient's observations.

But Caitlin didn't find it funny. Not today. Not as she might once have tried to do.

'Scott, if you're sure about this...' she said, shifting her chair closer and forcing him to meet her eye.

'Do you really doubt it?' he murmured. She ignored him.

'Then tell me something.' Deliberately, she made the words as blunt as she could. 'In the years when we were together, were you faithful to me?'

'Faithful?' he echoed. 'I never know what people *mean* by that!' he grumbled.

'*I* know what I mean by it!'

'Well, then, of course I was! In *my* terms. I mean, it's not a yes-or-no answer. Just a physical thing that—'

'Did you sleep with anyone else, Scott? *That's* a yes-or-no answer.'

He didn't reply. But he didn't need to. He couldn't meet her eye, and that was answer enough.

'We won't be getting back together,' she told him crisply. 'And the moment you're out of here and stop feeling so sorry for yourself, you won't even want to.'

For half an hour, while she left the hospital, drove home and made herself some tea, she felt wonderfully free—far freer than she had when she'd broken their engagement eleven days ago.

She owed Scott nothing now. Saying the words aloud, she knew she'd heard them before.

From Angus.

Then she thought, I'd never have asked him about it if Angus hadn't said what he did. He told me. He was right. And I accused him of lying just to get what he wanted, when all along Scott's been the one to do that.

With shaking fingers, she picked up the phone and rang Angus. And rang him, and rang him, and rang him, and finally realised that she was too late. He'd said his flight on Qantas was in the afternoon, but he must have had last-minute errands to take him away from his flat for the past few hours, and by now he must be at the airport, or on the way there.

At which point, her insides twisting again, she decided that she simply couldn't bear it if he left before she'd had a chance to apologise, to tell him she knew now that he'd been right about Scott. And yet she still couldn't give him the commitment he had asked for. She needed breathing space. Not a

long-distance commitment to someone she'd known for little
more than two weeks.

'Wh-what time is your next flight from Sydney to Los
Angeles?' she asked the Qantas operator on the phone, almost
too impatient to wait for the reply.

'Three forty-five.'

'Thanks.'

An hour and ten minutes. And he'd probably get ready to
board about an hour before flight time. The airport wasn't far,
and parking a motorbike wasn't difficult. There was a
chance…just a chance…

And if they could *talk*. Somehow she felt that if only she
could apologise and they could talk once more… Then what?
She still didn't know.

But when she raced to the airport and saw him, she knew
it was too late. Carrying a small navy overnight bag, he was
just a few metres from the doors that led into Customs and
Immigration, beyond which no ticketless person could go, and
she was still quite a distance from him, separated from that
dark-haired, darkly clad figure by fifty metres of seething, suit-
case-laden humanity.

For one moment he actually turned and scanned the
crowded departure concourse, as if he had felt her eyes on
him, felt her desperation, and the image of his face in the
distance burned itself into her memory so that she knew she'd
always be able to see it that way with utter clarity. That ir-
regular, rather hawk-like nose, those dark eyes and roughly
planed cheeks, that beautiful, sculpted mouth. He didn't see
her, though, and after a moment he turned back again.

She called out to him. *'An-gus!'* But her voice was puny
against the din of half a dozen different tongues spoken by
several dozen people and the cacophony of luggage trolley
wheels, and he didn't hear her, or see her crazy waving and
jumping. She ran, darting from side to side, tripping painfully
over the sharp corner of a Louis Vuitton bag.

'Careful!' the bag's owner snapped in her wake as he examined the expensive item tenderly.

'I'm sorry,' she gabbled.

'You should be!'

'Angus… Wait!' she shouted again through cupped hands.

But he was in the doorway now… He was through it… He had disappeared, and she was too late.

She stopped, breathless, tears stinging her eyes like acid, her throat tightly closed and her chest aching sharply. Someone cannoned into her from behind and again snapped at her angrily. Caitlin scarcely noticed, even though she murmured again automatically, 'I'm sorry.'

She felt as flat as a burst balloon, uselessly craving that final contact with him, but then asked herself in a strangled undertone, 'What did I want from him, anyway? I still wasn't going to say yes to him, was I?'

The tension had sizzled between them in her flat yesterday. 'Would he have wanted another fraught scene in the middle of the airport, less than an hour before his flight? It's better this way. Better for both of us.'

Which didn't explain why tears blinded her all the way back to where her motorbike was parked, and why she had to spend fifteen minutes calming herself down before she felt in control enough to ride home.

CHAPTER TEN

MUM rang late the next night. *Very* late. Almost midnight. Caitlin had arrived home from work at twenty past eleven and was now in her nightgown.

'I know it's late, Caitlin.' If voices could have glowed, Mum's did. 'But I knew you'd want to hear. Rachel's had a baby boy!'

'What? That's…that's fabulous!'

'She had him at nine o'clock this evening. She got another infection—a silent one, this time, so she didn't realise—and her waters broke in the middle of the shopping centre this afternoon, but of course the little chap is only just over six weeks early and he's going to be fine, the doctors say.'

'That's wonderful! Are you phoning from Canberra?'

'Yes, Gordon phoned us from the hospital and we drove straight up. What a pity the Fergusons aren't back from their trip! And I hear Angus has winged off to America for several months as well.'

'And does the little bloke have a name?' Caitlin asked quickly.

'Archie.'

'Um…'

'Well, I know, I'm not wild about it either but he's so gorgeous…'

'You *always* think that, Mum.'

'And I'm always right,' she agreed complacently. 'So, Caitlin, do you have any days off? Will you and Erin come down?'

'I will. I'm off Wednesday, Thursday and Friday. But I expect Erin may wait.'

'Yes, she's only just settling back in.'

And when Caitlin sat in Rachel's room at Canberra's Holy Cross Private Hospital on Thursday afternoon and watched her cuddle her new baby boy, she had to echo her mother's opinion. Archie Oliver Gray *was* gorgeous.

Rachel obviously thought so. She could hardly take her eyes off him, and Caitlin was shocked at the pang of envy that coursed through her.

She wasn't the type of 1990s woman who wanted to delay having children well into her thirties, or who felt that she might ultimately decide against it altogether. She'd always wanted kids. Two. Maybe three.

And she'd had a vague timetable for it in her mind when she'd been engaged to Scott. He'd needed to finish his internship, decide on a speciality and commence his studies in that area. Three or four years, and she'd have liked to have started trying. If Scott had been more advanced in his career, she'd have wanted to try sooner.

Now, of course, all those plans were in the past and at times she felt frighteningly adrift...

Suddenly, Rachel and the baby blurred in her vision, and to her horror she felt hot tears splash down onto her hands. There was a word for this—overreacting!

I had a chance with Angus. He wanted it. I said no. I have no right to react like this!

And, please, don't look up, Rachel!

She did, though. Caitlin had realised from the beginning that her vivacious sister-in-law had a fairly sensitive emotional antenna in some areas. At the moment, she didn't know whether to hate it or be grateful.

'It'll happen for you,' came a quiet voice. 'Be patient! You're not even twenty-four yet.'

'February,' Caitlin sniffed. 'And I know you're right. But it's not that.'

'Is it Scott? Are you regretting what you did?'

'No, nothing like that.'

'There's something, though.'

'Yes, I've—it feels strange even to say it, but it's real—met someone else.' She had to talk about it. And who better than Angus's sister?

'That was quick,' Rachel teased gently.

'That was the problem,' she explained clumsily. 'It was too soon. And he couldn't wait. Then also, which is nagging at me, he told me something which I didn't believe at the time—but which I've found out since was true—and I didn't even have a chance to apologise for doubting him.'

Amazingly, Rachel seemed to have followed all this. 'You couldn't write?' she questioned.

'About something like that? Not—not when we parted so badly. He wanted an answer, and I was too scared to give it to him. We fought about it. He accused me of— Well, I just didn't have the courage. Not when I've seen Erin's situation, and Sarah, a friend of mine—what's going on for her, too.' She took a breath after the garbled words and went on more clearly. 'I try to draw some sort of *answer* out of what's happening for both of them. Guidance. An example. You know what I mean. And I can't.'

'Listen, Caitlin, you haven't exactly given me the blow-by-blow details, but one thing I'm sure of is that when it comes to love,' Rachel urged seriously, 'don't take notice of anyone else! Whatever their situation is, it's not the same as yours because they're different people. The only two people who count are you and him. You've known him for…?'

'Just three—' She broke off and amended with deliberate vagueness, 'Well, a few weeks, though I—I guess I've known *of* him for longer.'

'Then perhaps it took more courage for you to say no. Why was he in such a rush? And why is it too late to apologise for doubting him?'

'Because— Oh, I can't tell you. I can't!'

She knew Rachel was watching her. And she knew Rachel was no fool. She was Angus's sister after all.

'Caitlin, I'm adding things up... It's not...? Is it because he's gone away?' Rachel questioned quietly.

'Here we are!' Mum breezed into the room with Dad and half a truckload of flowers.

'Caitlin, do close that blind for me now, would you?' Rachel jumped in quickly. 'Then go and ask the nurse at the desk about—about vases.'

Bless her! Caitlin thought a minute or two later as she stood in the visitors' cloakroom, splashing her tear-stained face. Bless her!

Although if she'd known what Rachel had passionately scribbled, with much underlining and exclamation marks, in a card to her brother Angus later that day, she might have rescinded the words.

'I've got some sad news, Caitlin,' Laurel Thompson told her on Wednesday morning, six days later, just before lunch.

'Oh, what?' Though she had a sinking feeling that she knew. It had been a big summer for news so far. 'There is a season...' she thought, suppressing a sigh. An engagement and more than one heart broken, a birth, and now...

'I've just been on the phone to Newby House,' Laurel said. 'Mrs Reid died this morning.'

'Yes? So very quickly? I know that's a blessing in so many ways but...' She trailed off.

'Stevie was there, sitting right by her and holding her hand. It was very peaceful. She just...*left*, apparently, as they sometimes do. According to the nurse, Stevie didn't even realise it had happened for some minutes. The funeral will be on Friday. I think one of us should—'

'Yes, of course. I'll go,' Caitlin came in. 'I'd like to. I admired and liked Mrs Reid so much. And Stevie's going to sing. I'd like to hear that.'

'Will you need to switch rosters?' Laurel frowned. 'I can't remember.'

'No, I have an afternoon anyway. Presumably it's in the morning?'

'Yes, at ten-thirty. Caitlin, this isn't what's been making you so down lately, is it?'

'I…' She shook her head, then laughed in dismay. 'Has it been…that obvious?'

'Only occasionally. You're not wearing it for all to see, if you're afraid of that. But I knew you'd grown fond of Mrs Reid, and—'

'No, it's not Mrs Reid. And I'm glad it's not too obvious. It's…something personal. I'd rather not—'

'Then don't.' Laurel patted her shoulder. 'I won't pry. I was just concerned.'

'I know. But don't be. I'll work it out.'

With time.

It was Angus, of course. She just couldn't help wondering, couldn't help mentally rearranging the past so that their mad, impossible relationship could have worked out.

If Scott and I hadn't been engaged, I'd have had time to trust how much Angus meant to me. I wouldn't have spent all my time fighting it, fighting *him*. If Angus had only told me sooner what he knew about Scott. And yet perhaps he was right not to. He *cared* about how I'd react. Why didn't I see that when he said it? It was there in his face and voice, only the words were such a shock I just couldn't believe them.

Oh, I keep seeing his face that day at the airport, scanning the crowd. If he'd seen me, come up to me, taken me in his arms and kissed me, I might have known *then* that I should trust it as he was telling me to. I might have found the courage that he had.

But, no, it had been doomed from the start. You can't meet that way, with the clock running and all that suspicious chemistry and another person involved. I'll have to accept that it just wasn't meant to be.

The sense of loss was acute, and increased rather than diminished. She knew Rachel had guessed but was glad they hadn't had a further chance to talk about it. She didn't want Rachel to know quite how hard it was. Rachel would only point out that Angus was coming back in May...

But May was four months away, and when you'd only known someone for two weeks four months was a long time. Anything could happen.

The city sang in the heat on Friday morning when Caitlin arrived at St Luke's Uniting Church for Betty Reid's funeral. The old stone building was cool, though, and nearly filled with mourners, many of whom were fellow multiple sclerosis sufferers and their carers, members of the support group Betty and Stevie had attended. There were several wheelchairs sitting in the side aisles next to the first few rows of pews, and a group of women who Caitlin guessed must be from Stevie's country music band.

Some rows in front of her she saw Dr Julius Marr's tall, loose-limbed figure and followed his gaze still further ahead to where Stevie stood at the front with some older men and women who must be her aunts and uncles. Stevie looked calm, though the two sheets of paper in her hand were rapidly getting crumpled.

They had become even more so by the time Stevie stood up and came forward to sing.

'Mum asked for this,' she said. 'I wrote it for her the week before she died, so she's heard it before. I hope and believe she can hear it now. Please excuse me, everyone, if I get emotional.'

She sang. It was a country ballad, its words simple and unpretentious, but made truly meaningful by the depth of feeling behind them, and its tune quite haunting in Stevie's rich voice. The acoustics of the church were wonderful, and despite her diminutive size she was able to fill the place with sound.

Her voice cracked twice and Caitlin had to fight back her own tears. She didn't want to cry, feeling that it would devalue the tears of those here who had really known Betty Reid and who were grieving deeply. She could only claim respect, not grief, for someone who had been her patient for just a few short days.

Dr Marr was watching Stevie again, his strongly chiselled face lifted and his expression intent. He's nervous for her, Caitlin realised. She's the only person he's thinking about. Look at him, coiled as an animal about to spring. He knows she doesn't want to break down now.

And Stevie didn't. When she reached the end of the song, the last note of it lay in the air for a moment and then there was silence, although for one distracted second Caitlin expected wild, tumultuous applause. She saw Dr Marr's shoulders relax and his limbs loosen, and knew he'd let out the breath he must have been holding in tension.

The service continued in the experienced hands of the rector and concluded a few minutes later. Mrs Reid had chosen cremation, and had asked that her ashes be scattered in the garden at her home where she had once worked so happily.

Many of the mourners were going back there for a quiet gathering, but Caitlin didn't want to intrude on this. She met up with Stevie on the steps of the church and the latter thanked her for coming in a rather mechanical way which told Caitlin how much she still had to struggle to get through this.

'Your song was just right,' she said to the older woman.

'Thanks. And thanks for helping me find the courage to sing it.'

Julius Marr asked carefully, 'What next, Stephanie? Do you have any plans?'

'Not yet,' she answered, turning to him with a distracted half-smile. His hand was poised to touch her back, but didn't connect in the end. 'Life goes on. But I want to wait before making any big changes. It's been impossible to think ahead until now.'

More people crowded around, Dr Marr stepped back and Caitlin squeezed Stevie's hand, said goodbye and left.

'How was it?' Laurel asked her later that day at work.

'Lots of people. Mrs Reid's brother said some good things, and Stevie's song was wonderful.'

'And how is Stevie?'

'Well, as she said, life goes on…'

And that's how I feel, too, Caitlin realised as she turned to some paper-work. Life goes on, but how do I start?

She began to plot some wildly improbable nursing escapades overseas and considered switching some time in the future to some other nursing speciality. Midwifery? All those darling babies, like Erin saw all day? No! Dermatology, then? 'Nine to five, and no one dies,' went the litany from doctors who favoured this field. But that degree of regularity seemed like a negative feature at the moment when she was so restless.

At some level, though, even as she was making these wild plans, she knew she didn't intend to carry them through. She wasn't really unhappy with Sydney or surgery…or even summer.

I just want— But she stopped, stubbornly not allowing herself to say his name.

And when she saw him—Angus—standing by the lift that night at eleven as she left the ward, she was quite convinced at first that she was hallucinating.

Then he smiled—smiled gorgeously with his beautiful mouth, making all his laugh lines crease from jaw to forehead, showing his straight white teeth, raising his strongly drawn brows, lighting up his dark eyes so that his whole rough-hewn face glowed—and her knees started to shake. She'd known him for two weeks, and been apart from him for nearly that much more, but he was as familiar now as if she'd loved him her whole life.

'A-Angus? It can't be you!' Even her voice shook.

'Yes, I feel a bit that way myself…' he grinned '…after fourteen hours and twenty minutes non-stop from Los Angeles. I'm not convinced that it's me at all. Could you, please, help me make sure?'

He held out his arms and she went into them as if she were coming home. His touch soothed away aches she hadn't known she had, and when she laid her head against his chest and heard his heartbeat there it was like beautiful music.

'All right,' he said after a moment. 'Panic's off. It *is* me, isn't it? And I'm going to kiss you, Caitlin. But not here. Let's go.'

He released her then slid his hand down her arm to lace her fingers in his and reached out with the other hand to summon the lift. At his feet she now noticed the same navy blue overnight bag she'd seen him with twelve days ago as he'd disappeared through that horrible door marked Ticketed Passengers Only.

'Why aren't you in Los Angeles?' she asked him helplessly. She also wondered why they were taking the lift *up*, but at the moment that mystery was of less urgent concern.

'Because I got a very angry and dramatic card from Rachel several days ago, sent by international express mail, announcing that she was never going to forgive me or, barring certain steps taken on my part, speak to me ever again. And I'm quite fond of my sister, odd as it may seem, so I decided I'd better do as I was told.'

'I—I don't understand,' she answered with a helpless laugh.

They reached the top floor and got out, to find a hospital maintenance man awaiting them. 'I can't give you more than fifteen minutes, I'm afraid, Dr Sinclair,' he warned, 'And if my beeper goes off…'

'I've dealt with inopportune beepers before,' Angus said. 'Thanks. I'll owe you for this.'

'No worries.' The man unlocked an unobtrusive and unmarked door near the lift then took out a small can of rust-remover and began to touch up some areas around the railing of the emergency stairs just opposite. 'Told you there was a job up here I'd been meaning to get to.'

'Um, Angus, you have to explain better than that. You're *here*!' She was following him through the door and up the last half-flight of stairs to the roof as she spoke. It was impossibly wonderful just to be with him, touching him and hearing his voice, but he'd hardly begun to answer her question! He *should* be in Los Angeles!

He looked back at her. 'We had rather a nice time when last we stood on a roof together, if you recall,' he said lightly. 'I…hoped you might wish to repeat the experience.'

'Not *here* on a roof. Here in Sydney!'

'You don't like the roof? You'd rather go—?'

'Angus, I can't think of any place I'd rather be than this roof,' she told him impatiently, 'but—'

'OK,' he soothed. 'Can I get to it in my own way? Proper apologies often take a long run-up.'

'*Apologies?*'

'Can I finish telling you about Rachel's card?'

'Please!'

'Where was I up to?'

'That she was never going to forgive you or speak to you.'

'Yes, for hurting you the way I had and for calling your answer to me cowardice. She said it was *far* more courageous of you to say no to what I asked than to say yes, under the circumstances. She said it showed your integrity and your good sense and your understanding of what a man's and a woman's commitment to each other really means and—'

'Quite a long card!'

'Yes, and almost illegible, there was so much underlining, but Caitlin, sweet darling, she was absolutely right about all of it. And, as all seats in economy and business class were sold out, for the only days I could get off over the next few weeks, I've just had to purchase a very expensive first-class airline ticket in order to rectify the situation.'

'You mean…'

'I apologise. I pushed and I didn't listen and I flung that nasty truth about Scott at you for all the nefarious reasons you accused me of.'

'But you were right about it,' she said quietly. 'He started talking about us getting back together, and I challenged him on it and—'

'He admitted it?'

'No! He *didn't* admit it, which was even more telling. He tried to gloss over it and play it down, and when I asked him a direct question that he couldn't wriggle out of he couldn't meet my eyes, and I knew. And I started to see what a dilemma that must have been for you, especially at first when you thought I really loved him.'

'Yes, it coloured those days over Christmas very strongly.'

'And it was why you tortured me with that Devil's advocate game of yours at Kiama on our way up to Sydney. You wanted to know if I played the field a bit myself. If maybe I knew about it already, and didn't mind.'

'I should apologise for that, too. Again, I bulldozed you.'

'No! I can't see how else it all could have happened. Or

what you could have done differently. You've…' she smiled up at him, tears welling in her eyes suddenly, '…had a wasted trip, Angus. You didn't need to apologise at all!'

'Not even for questioning your courage?'

'Not even for that. I—I've spent every waking moment for the past two weeks wishing I'd had it, Angus,' she admitted in a low voice, staring quickly down again.

'And do you have it now?' he whispered.

'Yes. Oh, yes…'

'Enough now, my love, to say yes to our future together with no doubts and no hesitations?'

'None at all. Rachel made me see that I was bringing too many other people into it. Scott, and Erin, and what was going on with a friend of mine. She said the only people that counted were you and me, and I realised it was true, and then I knew what I felt.'

'Can you come over to Los Angeles, then? You were right, four months and thousands of miles is too much. We need to be together for at least part of that time. Can you take some leave at some point, even if it's only for a week—?'

'Actually, I have a full four weeks owing, and with accrued days off I could probably put together a bit more…'

'More than four weeks! Then *would* you, because the thought of doing without you for another fourteen weeks when this is all so new is giving me vertigo?'

'That could be the roof,' she suggested seriously.

'*Answer* me!'

'Oh, Angus, I don't need to, do I? Isn't it obvious?' she said rather shakily, leaning against him and rubbing her cheek against the warmth of his neck. 'But if you want to hear it, then, yes! Oh, yes! These twelve days since you left have been so hard and horrible. I thought I'd lost you, and to lose you while feeling I'd never really had you at all was…' She shuddered. 'The whole thing felt like a dream, and I thought I was mad to mind so much and a fool not to have seen everything clearly before.'

She reached up to stroke his face then gasped as his lips fell hard against her mouth and clung there. His face was deliciously rough. He hadn't shaved since before the flight. She ran her lips hungrily over his cheeks then tasted him again and wrapped her arms around his strong back to feel the heat of him pressed against her from chest to knees.

A sea-tanged breeze blew mildly from the water, and they were high enough to see the ocean from here across the tiled roofs of the houses, painted a pale luminous blue by the street lights and the moon. Maroubra Beach and Lurline Bay curved to the south-east of the hospital, to the south-west lay Botany Bay and to the north they could see as far as Bondi.

Tomorrow we'll go to the beach, she decided hazily and happily. I love the way he is in the water…

Then she suddenly remembered. 'When do you have to go back? When did you *get* here?'

'I got here…the plane touched down…at precisely ten past ten tonight. It was fifteen minutes early.'

'But it's only twenty past eleven now!'

'I only brought carry-on luggage. I went straight through customs and into a taxi. It didn't take long to get to the hospital at this time of night.'

'But how did you know I'd even be there?'

'I rang the ward from the plane. Spoke to Brooke Peters, though I didn't tell her where I was calling from or why I was asking about who was on.'

'But…from the *plane*?'

'You can do that these days. Mind you, it isn't cheap!'

'I bet it's not!' she responded happily. It was nice to know that a man was prepared to throw his money around like that purely for the pleasure of her company. Spur-of-the-moment first-class airline tickets, satellite phone calls…

'And I have to go back tomorrow night,' he finished heavily. 'The flight's at seven.'

'So soon!' It was a heart-felt wail.

'Caitie, it was hard enough to wangle enough time off so I'd actually have the opportunity to leave the airport!'

'Then I guess I'd better apply for that four weeks' leave first thing Monday morning,' she said weakly, unable to stand the thought of prolonging the bereft, empty feeling she'd been living with for the past twelve days.

'Do you think you could get it for February?'

'I'll try.'

'And we can spend the next two weeks phoning each other with suggestions about what to do with the time…although I do have several ideas already,' he growled seductively.

'At the moment,' she confessed, 'I'm more interested in your ideas about what we can do with the next eighteen hours.' So short! Painfully so!

'As to that,' he said against her lips, 'I'm afraid I feel quite devoid of imagination at the moment. All I can think of is kissing you, eating something, kissing you again, going a lot further than kissing, lying beside you and…' he turned his head away and yawned against the back of his hand, '…falling asleep.'

'In that order?'

'In that order first, and then with a random repetition of the pattern for as long as we've got.'

'I wish it were eighteen days…'

'Should we spend some of our eighteen hours telling your family, do you think? Or mine?'

'Let's not,' she begged tenderly. 'Not yet.'

'Not even Rachel?' he teased.

'Not even Rachel. Although somehow,' she said with a slow smile, 'I think she knew exactly the response she'd get from you with that card of hers. And she's probably told Mum, and they're probably already planning the wedding!'

Angus groaned. 'No doubt you're right. Does your mother favour large weddings, do you know?'

'She favours any sort of wedding as long as it ends in a marriage. We could dress in plastic bags and stand up together in a garbage can, as far as she's concerned, as long as there were rings and vows and a signed certificate.'

'That's been your girlhood dream, has it, a garbage-can wedding?'

'Well, no, perhaps just a tad more upmarket than that,' she acknowledged.

'Whatever you want,' he told her, nuzzling his lips against her hair and threatening thereby to distract her totally from the subject at hand...whatever it was. 'Although,' he added, after a delectable exploration of her mouth, 'I wouldn't mind having a say in your ring. We can choose one together when you come over.'

'Yes, we won't do it tomorrow. After that first-class plane ticket of yours, I might want to wait until your coffers are replenished a bit,' she teased, looking out across the ocean, leaning back into his strong chest and thinking that if wishing could get you what you wanted, she'd be there now, in Los Angeles, with him, the two weeks of waiting which now seemed to stretch ahead so endlessly already consigned to the past.

But that was crazy—short-sighted—and she rebelled against such a defeatist attitude. They had eighteen hours together right now, didn't they? And every minute of them was going to be perfect. She was absolutely *not* going to waste their hours together in worrying about their weeks apart!

Pulling him imperiously into her arms, cupping his fatigue-roughened face between her palms and sweetly exploring his beautiful mouth, she made very good use of several of those minutes then and there. He groaned and responded with gratifying enthusiasm.

But finally there came a discreet cough behind them and it was Angus's very amenable maintenance man, come to lock up his door.

'Where exactly shall we go once we're out of the lift, then?' Angus asked her, still holding her close as they walked towards the roof exit.

And in a positive mist of happiness, living every second to the full just as she had vowed to do, feeling the heat of him pressed against her side and the dark vibration of his voice so close to her ear, Caitlin could only answer with a vague, blissful smile, 'I'm sorry, Angus, but at the moment I just can't think that far ahead...'

MILLS & BOON®

MISTLETOE
Magic

Three favourite Enchanted™ authors
bring you romance at Christmas.

Three stories in one volume:

A Christmas Romance
BETTY NEELS

Outback Christmas
MARGARET WAY

Sarah's First Christmas
REBECCA WINTERS

Published 19th November 1999

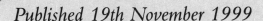

Available at most branches of WH Smith, Tesco,
Martins, Borders, Easons, Volume One/James Thin
and most good paperback bookshops

10...9...8...

As the clock struck midnight three single people became instant parents...

Millennium baby

Kristine Rolofson
Baby, It's Cold Outside

Bobby Hutchinson
One-Night-Stand Baby

Judith Arnold
Baby Jane Doe

Celebrate the Millennium with these three heart-warming stories of instant parenthood

Available from 24th December

FREE
2 BOOKS
AND A SURPRISE GIFT!

We would like to take this opportunity to thank you for reading this Mills & Boon® book by offering you the chance to take TWO more specially selected titles from the Medical Romance™ series absolutely FREE! We're also making this offer to introduce you to the benefits of the Reader Service™—

★ FREE home delivery
★ FREE monthly Newsletter
★ FREE gifts and competitions
★ Exclusive Reader Service discounts
★ Books available before they're in the shops

Accepting these FREE books and gift places you under no obligation to buy; you may cancel at any time, even after receiving your free shipment. Simply complete your details below and return the entire page to the address below. *You don't even need a stamp!*

YES! Please send me 2 free Medical Romance books and a surprise gift. I understand that unless you hear from me, I will receive 4 superb new titles every month for just £2.40 each, postage and packing free. I am under no obligation to purchase any books and may cancel my subscription at any time. The free books and gift will be mine to keep in any case.

M9EC

Ms/Mrs/Miss/Mr ....Initials ....
BLOCK CAPITALS PLEASE

Surname ....

Address ....

....

....Postcode ....

Send this whole page to:
UK: FREEPOST CN81, Croydon, CR9 3WZ
EIRE: PO Box 4546, Kilcock, County Kildare (stamp required)

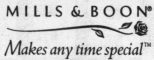

MILLS & BOON®

Makes any time special™

Bestselling themed romances brought back to you by popular demand

Each month By Request brings you three full-length novels in one beautiful volume featuring the best of the best.

So if you missed a favourite Romance the first time around, here is your chance to relive the magic from some of our most popular authors.

Look out for

Christmas Presents

in December 1999

featuring Penny Jordan, Anne McAllister and Sally Wentworth